UNSEEN MAGIC

AN AGENTS OF MAGIC URBAN FANTASY NOVEL

SARAH BIGLOW

UNSEEN MAGIC Copyright © 2022 by Sarah Biglow.

All rights reserved. No part of this book may be used or reproduced in any manner whatsoever without written permission except in the case of brief quotations embodied in critical articles or reviews.

This book is a work of fiction. Names, characters, businesses, organizations, places, events and incidents either are the product of the author's imagination or are used fictitiously. Any resemblance to actual persons, living or dead, events, or locales is entirely coincidental.

If you enjoy this book, please consider leaving a review.

For information contact; www.sarah-biglow.com

Edited by: Under Wraps Publishing Services

Cover Design by: Deranged Doctor Design

Large Print Hardcover ISBN: 978-1-955988-49-0

10 9 8 7 6 5 4 3 2 1

JUNE 3, 2019

ONE

I'd spent so much time being invisible, stepping into the spotlight made my skin itch. Yet, I'd let my class talk me into being the spokesperson for graduation. I wasn't good at speeches, or dealing with crowds, but maybe that was why they'd tapped me for this gig. They knew I needed to be pushed outside of my comfort zone to prove I had what it took to do the job we'd all trained for. Learning the theories and the scenarios were easy. Hell, training to shoot a gun wasn't that difficult. Though dealing with people and talking them down, that terrified me. I'd never been great at interpersonal skills and I forever worried I'd say the wrong thing.

Which probably explained why two hours before graduation, I'd sequestered myself on the shooting range. Alone, I could focus and give myself a little magic boost to calm my nerves. For so many years, the scent of my magic had been a reminder that it had rebelled against me, making me literally invisible to the people around me. But I'd worked hard the last few years to regain control—to be seen when I wanted. Even now, when it welled up around me, what should be the soothing scent of lavender sparked a moment of panic that it was going to rise up and swallow me whole again.

"Why am I not surprised you're hiding out here?" a familiar voice called from behind me.

The sudden intrusion on my solitude made me jump and set down the unloaded weapon on the booth in front of me. The protective earmuffs hung around my neck. The voice made me picture an old friend as I turned to see soon-to-be Special Agent Perri Frasier standing in the doorway. We'd bonded a lot during the academy.

"Because you know me too well," I offered and took the earmuffs off. At least the version of me I'd let my classmates see over the last five months. Magic was a secret to be guarded and I couldn't go blabbing about it to just anyone.

She sauntered up beside me and leaned against the barrier between my stall and the next. She was heavier set than me—which wasn't hard—and about half a foot taller. I had seen her take down guys twice her size with precision. There weren't many other people I'd want to have my back in a mundane fight.

"Have you even decided what you're going to say?" she prodded, tucking loose strands of dirty blonde hair behind her ear.

I shrugged and shoved my hands in my pockets. "I mean, what they expect me to say. Stuff about how it was tough getting where we are, that we've got a long road ahead, and that we'll get there, because we've got each other."

"Well, that's something. Then again, no one expects you to be a great orator, Kay," she said with a smirk.

"Glad I won't disappoint anyone then," I quipped with a smile.

"Do you think you'll head back up north afterward?"

I hadn't admitted my plans to anyone, but I was eager to go somewhere new after I finished the academy. There were things and people I'd been avoiding back home in Boston, namely my parents. So, I'd put in requests to go anywhere else. Hell, I would settle in Texas if that's where they decided I needed to go.

"I'll go where they send me," I answered, purposely avoid her question.

She clucked her tongue at me. "You're hiding from more than just graduation," she surmised.

I rolled my eyes. "Don't profile me."

"Habit. And I'm not sorry. Whatever drama you've got going back home is going to impact you on the job one day. It's better to clear that up now before it festers."

I sighed. "It's just family stuff." It wasn't a total lie. I did have family shit waiting back home. I didn't want the pressure of having to reconnect with parents whose own expectations of their then-teenage daughter had turned her into a Whisperer. In a few short hours, I might be Special Agent Kayla Rogers, but even she had limits on the pain she could endure.

"Aren't your parents going to be here?"

I shook my head. "We aren't really on speaking terms. They didn't show up for my college graduation either, so I don't see why this would be any different."

"They might surprise you." The certainty in her tone caught my attention.

What does she know?

My newly-trained investigator brain told me to press her, to coax the information from her. Except I was still too nervous about getting through graduation to push her any more.

"What about you? Where are you hoping

to end up?" I turned the topic to her instead—good old deflection.

"I put in my top request to stick around Virginia."

"Well maybe we'll get lucky, and both end up here," I said with what I intended to be a hopeful note in my voice.

Perri wrapped her arm around my shoulders and pulled me in for a one-armed hug. "I'm telling you, Kay, parents aren't that scary."

That's because her parents were decent people. She wasn't trying to outrun a past that still threatened to ruin everything she'd worked for. Although, given that I was one step away from being handed a badge and gun, most of that past seemed firmly rooted in my rearview. The criminal activity at the very least was something I'd never touch again.

I couldn't shake the sense of foreboding that tugged at my subconscious. It whispered there were things that I couldn't escape, no matter how fast or far I fled. Somehow I'd managed to silence those voices all the way through school and the academy. I refused to let them get in my way now. Not when I was so close to starting a new chapter of my life. One where I dictated what happened, not other people and most certainly not my magic.

MY THROAT WENT dry as I sat in the front row, listening to the Director of the FBI welcome everyone to the ceremony. My fellow recruits sat around me in silence. Some were stoic, looking straight ahead while others craned their necks to see what family had come to show their support. I glanced down at the notes I'd hastily scrawled on a note card, so I didn't completely embarrass myself.

"You've got this," Perri said beside me. It wasn't a secret that she had been picked by our instructors to receive a special award for her skills in physical fitness.

Branson Slattery, a rail-thin black man with a buzzcut and a gaze that could rival the Mona Lisa was set to receive an award for academics. Which meant he sat on my other side. I'd earned the spot in the middle, because I was the class spokesperson.

"She's right. You're going to kill it," he offered, patting my shoulder.

I swallowed a time or two to get the parched feeling off my tongue as I waited for my cue to take the stage. I didn't have to wait long. The Director glanced my way and said, "And now we will have remarks from the graduating class spokesperson, Kayla Rogers."

A few whistles went up from my fellow recruits as I took the stage. I set my notes on the lectern and gripped the sides with both hands until my knuckles turned pale. Gazing out at the mass of faces, I tried not to get lost in them. I briefly scanned the crowd, half expecting to see my parents in there somewhere. Perri had been so certain they'd make an appearance that when I didn't pick them out, disappointment washed over me.

Exhaling slowly, I turned my gaze to Perri. It would be easier if I pretended I was talking just to her. She gave me an encouraging smile and for a moment, I was reminded of yet another person who'd set me on this journey. One I intended to honor with this speech if all went well.

"So, five months ago, most of us showed up at the academy with hopes and dreams of being some pretty kick-ass federal agents," I began. The statement earned a few chuckles from the crowd. "I don't think any of us expected it to be easy, but I know I never anticipated it would lead me to do so much soul searching."

Hot tears pricked at the backs of my eyes, but I held strong. I wasn't going to cry. Not when I was supposed to be projecting strength and confidence. "I came into this journey, because a friend put her life on the line to protect people, to protect me, and she made the ultimate sacrifice. Her bravery inspired me to do better with my life. To pay back what she did for me."

I paused to collect myself. It had been nearly two years since Ezri had died to save all of magic and it still felt fresh. Like she was supposed to walk through the door any minute, asking for my help. I'd been so snarky the first time we'd met and reluctant to break the rules for her even when little girls' lives were on the line. I'd been unsure of who I was back then. It took losing her to realize I needed to regain control of my life once and for all.

"We've all been through some rough patches over the last few months. Training exercises pushed us out of our comfort zones and tested our mental and physical strength." My voice grew louder, firmer as I spoke. I didn't even need to glance down at my notes now. "And I know there were days that more than a few of us worried we'd break under the responsibility of taking those weapons onto the streets."

I gestured to the table just off the stage where our firearms and ammunition waited. "But we've made it. We're graduating and we're about to represent the best of what this country stands for. We're going to be fair and just. We're going to protect the citizens wherever we land. And we know we're not going to be alone when we do it, because no matter where we go, we'll always have the bonds we built here."

I pocketed the note card and stepped back from the lectern. Perri beamed up at me and even Branson gave me an approving look. His gaze followed me as I stepped down from the stage and returned to my seat. I sank into the leather backing as the collective's attention turned to bestowing honors on the award recipients.

At least now I had time to breathe and really take in the fact I was about to graduate from the fucking FBI Academy. I turned to take in the crowd behind the graduating class. I spotted our instructors taking up the first row with other agents peppered in, identified by their flak jackets and badges. There were the obligatory relatives for most of my colleagues and I thought I caught movement at the very back of the crowd. They were too quick for me to catch their face properly, but my gut told me I should recognize them.

"Kayla Rogers," the Director called my name.

I was so zoned out I hadn't realized we'd already moved on to receiving our badges and credentials. Normally it would have gone alphabetically, but being voted spokesperson meant I got to go first. I returned to the stage, took the badge and credentials, and slid the chain over my head. The Director offered his hand and I shook it.

As I started to pull back, he leaned in and whispered, "Good speech, Agent."

"Thank you, sir," I replied, and he relinquished my hand.

I returned down the stairs and back to my seat. Perri and Branson followed, and then the rest of the class in alphabetical order until Lilian Zang sported her credentials.

"I present to you the graduating class of 2019," the Director said.

One of the instructors gestured for us to follow him to the table to receive our service weapons. Even though I'd put in countless hours on the shooting range, slipping the weapon into a holster on my hip still felt foreign.

A second instructor began circulating amongst our group, passing out envelopes with duty assignments. She bypassed Perri and I, and went searching for Branson. He'd already retreated to his family. His parents and four siblings clustered around him, inspecting his badge and credentials with pride.

"You were selling yourself short before," Perri chided, nudging my shoulder. "That speech was great. You almost made me cry."

"I kind of surprised myself, too."

"You never talked about your friend before," she added.

"It's kind of a touchy subject. She was a cop back home. Line of duty death," I said. Every word of it was true. Perri didn't need to know that Ezri Trenton had been the Savior and her line of duty death didn't have anything to do with her job as a police detective.

"The fact you chose the same line of work says a lot about how much she must have meant to you," Perri offered as the instructor came back and handed her an envelope.

"I like to think she'd be proud of me," I said, tracking the instructor's movements as she approached the instructor who'd passed out our guns. Everyone else, but me held an envelope now. Pushing the unease down, I turned back to Perri. "So, the suspense is killing me. Where'd you end up?"

She slid her finger beneath the flap and pulled out a folded sheet of paper. I spotted the official FBI letterhead at the top. "You have been assigned to the Washington D.C. field office," she read aloud.

"Not quite Virginia, but pretty damn close," I noted.

"Yeah. I'll take it." She looked around. "Why haven't you gotten your assignment yet?"

Before I could answer, someone tapped my shoulder. I turned to see the instructor who'd been handing out assignments standing there looking solemn. "Agent Rogers, I need you to come with me."

Every instinct screamed at me, warning something was wrong. That all of this was about to fall apart before it even started. I did my best to keep a calm demeanor as I followed her out of the room into a side hallway. The Director stood there, like he'd been waiting for me. Without warning, the instructor left me there. No explanation.

"Sir, I don't mean to complain, but I'm a little confused. Everyone else received their duty assignments."

"Except you," he finished.

I nodded. "Did I do something wrong?"

He shook his head, his lips breaking out into a smile. "On the contrary. You were slated for the D.C. office, but a Senior Field Agent requested you by name for a joint taskforce. You report for duty tomorrow morning."

"What?" My voice pitched up a few notes. In that moment, my brain tried to process the excitement that I'd been about to stick with Perri post-graduation and the disappointment that it was dashed by some nameless agent I'd never met. A little bit of excitement tried to sneak in at the prospect of being tapped for such a prestigious assignment straight out of the academy.

"You're getting on a plane in thirty minutes, Agent Rogers."

"Where am I going?"

"Boston."

So much for avoiding a trip home.

TWO

Cramming clothes into a bag ten minutes later, I couldn't help feeling torn. Getting tapped for a taskforce was a big deal, especially right out of the academy. I didn't have any field experience for one thing. For all I knew, I'd end up doing coffee runs for the other agents and local police liaisons. But what had I done to deserve it? As I zipped up the bag, the door behind me whined on its hinges. Perri stood there, worry lines creasing her forehead.

"I'm fine," I told her.

"What happened? You disappeared and now I find you packing."

The concern in her tone was touching. She assumed I'd gotten bad news. "Yeah, I got detailed to a taskforce back home. They expect me on a plane in twenty minutes."

"Seriously?" her concern turned to excitement as she flung herself at me. "That's amazing. No one gets tapped for big assignments like that right after graduation. I mean, six months or a year down the line, maybe, if you're lucky."

"Why don't we hold that assessment until I know what I'm actually doing?"

Perri stepped back and straightened, falling into a more professional posture. "You're right. Well, I'm sure whatever it is, you'll do great. They wouldn't have picked you if they didn't believe in you."

"Thanks for the vote of confidence," I replied, checking my phone to make sure I wasn't late.

Perri clapped me on the shoulder and

started for the door. "Just out of curiosity, where were you supposed to be headed?"

I couldn't hold back the smile. "D.C."

"Damn. Well, maybe once this taskforce is wrapped up, you'll head down my way."

I could only hope. We stood there in my dorm room for a few minutes longer before my phone beeped loudly with an incoming text. It wasn't a number I recognized.

"I'll let you go. You're going to kill it, Kay," Perri called with a wave.

I wished I could bottle some of her confidence. Even with all the strides I'd made in finding myself again, I still had doubts. I opened the text to see instructions on where to go to make my flight. Shouldering my bag, I left the place that had been my home for the last five months behind.

THE FLIGHT WAS LESS than an hour thanks to being on a government aircraft. I sat in the plush leather seat and stared out at the passing clouds, trying not to let the unknown tighten my nerves. I was a trained agent and could handle whatever was coming my way.

As the plane descended into a part of Logan Airport I'd never seen before, my stomach twisted itself into anxious knots. Or maybe it was just a choppier landing than I'd anticipated. I listened to the sounds of the plane settling, engine shutting off, and other systems powering down. No one was kicking me off, so I stayed put as long as possible.

When a man in a dark navy suit stepped aboard and approached, I knew my time was up. Standing I offered my hand. "Special Agent Rogers."

"Special Agent Duncan." He shook my hand briefly. "The head of the taskforce sent me to let you know you should report to headquarters tomorrow by eight o'clock sharp."

Whoever the head of this taskforce was had some serious pull if they could get other people to be their messenger. Checking the time, I realized I had the afternoon free. Free time wasn't something I'd counted on. Not when the Director had seemed so insistent that I be in Boston as soon as humanly possible.

"Can I ask why I'm not reporting there right now?" The words fell out of my mouth before I could stop them.

Duncan gave me a noncommittal look. "I can only pass along what I'm told. Sorry. Enjoy a little time in the city I guess."

Yeah, loads of fun being home.

I followed Agent Duncan off the plane and he led the way through back halls I suspected weren't for public knowledge until we were in baggage claim. He didn't offer to give me a ride anywhere. So, I hopped on the Silver Line back to South Station and the red line of the MBTA. Some things about being home were comforting. Blending into the mess of people riding public transit was one of them. As I sat there in a train hurtling toward the center of the city, I relaxed. It was enough for the mental walls I'd been building to keep my magic in check to weaken and for some of it to seep through the cracks. The scent of lavender tickled my nose and I looked down to find my left hand had turned invisible.

I pulled back on the urge to sink into that invisibility until my hand returned. Maybe I'd been too focused on the mundane parts of my life, neglected to give my magic the attention it needed. If only there was someone who could help with that. As I stepped off the train at Park Street station, my phone rang with yet another unknown number.

I hit the green 'Accept' button, but faltered on how to answer the call. I settled on, "Hello?"

"Hey Kayla." Kevin's voice didn't carry the usual crackle of calling from a prison landline.

"Kev? What's going on? What number is this?" My boyfriend, who'd spent the last two years in prison was a model inmate. So, thoughts that he'd obtained an illegal prison phone tightened the muscles in my shoulders. He'd been locked up for killing five people. Except it hadn't been by choice. He'd felt compelled to confess even though he'd been under duress the whole time. There was small comfort in knowing the real mastermind behind the murders was also rotting in a cell.

"Don't panic, okay?" That was never a good way to preface a conversation. "Some things happened while you were away."

"Kevin, what the hell is going on? Just tell me."

"I got paroled."

The words sounded foreign to my ears. He shouldn't have been eligible for parole for at least another couple years. My years of being distrustful of the system screamed at me to run away, because this was clearly a trap. "What? How?"

"I don't know. But they're letting me out."

I took the stairs to the street level two at a time and came up across from the church. People milled about and I sought a vacant stretch of grass where I could pace and process his words. I asked the obvious question as my feet wore down the grassy patch beneath my shoes. "When?"

"Today. Well, right now."

A flurry of new questions danced around

my brain as I continued to pace. *Did his mother know? Why was he telling me this news, especially if he didn't know I was back in the city? Who had secured him such an early parole? What did that unknown person or persons want from Kevin?*

"Oh. Wow."

"I know you're busy and heading off on a new adventure, but I was hoping we could talk."

"Is someone picking you up?"

"I told my mom, but she had to work. I'll figure something out."

"Stay put. I'll be there in ten minutes."

I hung up before he could start peppering me with questions. I scanned the street beyond and found a waiting cab. The driver looked surprised when I gave him the address, but pulled away from the curb and headed off without a word.

Today is not going at all how I planned.

"Can you wait here for just a minute?" I told the driver as I unbuckled the seatbelt and opened the door.

"What about the meter?" he grumbled.

"Don't worry, I'm going to pay you. I just need to pick someone up," I answered and shut the door.

I stopped short of entering the prison proper. Kevin stood by the front door waiting for me. I'd spent a lot of time visiting him here, but we'd never been able to do more than talk. We'd considered ourselves a couple—or at least I had—but we hadn't been able to share any of the physical intimacy that comes along with that label. I threw my arms around him and held on for dear life.

"What are you doing back in Boston?" His question came as a whisper in my ear.

"Work thing," I answered. I knew enough not to give him any more detail than that.

When I finally loosened my grip, he held me out at arm's length. "Suits look good on you."

I blushed and took his hand. "Come on, I've got a grumpy cabbie waiting for us."

The driver gave me a look of relief in the

rearview mirror when we slid into the back seat. "Where to now, Miss?"

I looked to Kevin. He leaned forward and said, "The common."

It seemed an odd destination, seeing as he'd spent five years as a stone statue in the park against his will, his own magic forcing him to be immobile. Maybe that's why we'd reconnected. I understood what it meant to have your magic revolt against you. It didn't hurt that I had a thing for him in college. I'd been drawn to how open he was with his magic back then. I longed for him to teach me to control my own power. But he hadn't noticed me. If he had, maybe he wouldn't have ended up as the Order of Samael's puppet.

Prison had aged Kevin, but not in the way most people came out looking grizzled, worn down. He'd filled out and the five o'clock shadow he wore now was kind of sexy. He looked more like a grown up than when we'd reentered each other's lives. The cab pulled up almost exactly where he'd picked me up and I tapped my credit card to the machine to pay.

I let Kevin lead the way. We wandered along the paths, side by side, but not holding hands. Part of me wanted to push for that touch I'd been craving for so long, but the rational part of me knew he needed time to adjust to the real world again.

"So, what did you want to talk about?" I prodded.

"It's going to be weird living with my mom again after all these years," he said, his gaze darting from the nearby trees to people walking their dogs on the other side of the path.

"You'll figure it out. I'm pretty sure she kept your room like a shrine. At least that's what Ezri said once."

He nodded in silence. "I'm not that person anymore."

"I don't know about that. You're a good guy who was trying to help someone he cared about get out of a bad situation." I was being generous in my description of his ex-girlfriend since she was the reason he'd been turned to stone.

"But I also did some pretty terrible things."

"That wasn't you. You know that. That asshole forced you. He threatened the people you loved."

"But I still did it, Kayla." He blew out a breath. "You'd think after two years, I'd have some sort of clarity about all of it. But here I am, still spinning my wheels. I took responsibility for my actions, because I thought it would help me heal. I'm not sure it did that."

I wanted to tell him that he was going to be fine, but I had no way of knowing that for sure. After all, a part of him had been stripped away. Sure, it was done to save him, but it still meant part of his identity was missing. "Have you talked to anyone about losing your magic?"

He let out a harsh laugh. "I didn't need the prison shrink thinking I was crazy."

"Maybe you should talk to someone. It's just a guess, but maybe part of why you feel like you're still struggling is because you haven't been able to deal with that loss."

"Maybe ..." A pause and then he said, "Know any good shrinks?"

I was about to respond that I knew a great one, but stopped. "The Authority has someone who does counseling. I'd start there."

He nodded again, this time shoving his hands in pockets. "I appreciate everything you've done for me, Kayla, since I went to prison. You spent more time with me than anyone could have asked for."

"I knew you needed a friendly face. I wanted to be there. And look, I know it's been a while, but I couldn't just move the training academy here."

He held up his hand, signaling I should shut up. "I'm not blaming you for living your life and following the path you set for yourself. I think it's great."

"I'm sensing a 'but,'" I replied and stopped walking.

"But I'm not in that same place. I don't know what my future holds. For one thing, finding a job as an ex-felon isn't exactly a walk in the park. I think you're right that I don't know who I am without magic. Who is Kevin Ellery, normal guy who doesn't have anything special about him?"

"He's a pretty great guy from what I've seen." My voice hitched. I knew what was coming and I was trying desperately to avoid it.

"I need time to find out if what you're seeing is the real me." He took my hands now. As much as I'd wanted that physical contact, my instincts told me to pull away now. "But I need to do it on my own. Not forever, but for a little while. I don't think we should see each other for a while."

I squeezed my eyes shut to keep the unshed tears at bay. "You're seriously doing this right now? Not even half an hour after you're a free man?"

"I didn't want to string you along," he replied.

"Like you haven't been for the last two years?" I snapped.

"I promise, it's not going to be forever," he

said and pulled me in for a light kiss on the lips before he let me go.

The gesture was pathetic and only made my anger swell. Lavender flared around me. I could tell even he noticed the shift in power, because he stepped away, stumbled a step even. He regained his footing and started off on a different branch of the path through the park. He didn't look my way again. In the back of my mind, I was already orchestrating all the ways I could accidentally-on-purpose run into him in my head. I was still a member of the Authority, I had reasons to be at Headquarters. His mom and I had become friendly. I usually dropped by for coffee every other weekend when I was around. But if he wanted me out of his life, so be it. From now on, he would be part of the 'old' Kayla—the one who didn't have control of her life.

"Get a grip," I scolded myself, pushing those thoughts down deep.

If Kevin wanted to break things off, let him. Maybe I was the only one who'd considered what we had a relationship. Maybe to him I was just the girl who made his days in prison less boring. As I headed for my own apartment, which I'd managed to scrape enough together to pay the rent in my absence, I tried —and failed—not to stew in the anger that a break-up brings. I reminded myself that I had come back home, not for him, but for my new life. I let the fact I'd been handpicked buttress my sense of self. I was worried about it before, but I should really be looking at it as a sign that I was important enough to keep tabs on. Someone out there wanted me and I was going to prove just how useful I could be.

JUNE 4, 2019

THREE

Even setting my alarm for six o'clock, my body woke me up at quarter to five. Sleeping in my own bed had done me some good, even if it had taken until nearly midnight to quiet my thoughts enough to sleep. A break-up wasn't exactly what I'd had in mind as a precursor to starting my new job.

I got up, showered, and studied my reflection in the mirror. Gone was the girl who'd dyed her hair in shades of purple as a way to be left alone. It attracted enough attention, so that other people decided they didn't want to have anything to do with the goth girl. It had served its purpose, but I was in the real world now, where appearances mattered in a different way. I needed to blend in with the people around me and to do that, I needed to look *normal*. It felt strange securing the gun holster to my hip, but a feeling I had to get used to. They'd drilled it into us at the academy that when you were on duty you had to know where your weapon was at all times. I needed to buy a lock box for my apartment.

I still had an hour before I needed to leave to make it to headquarters on time. Sitting around my apartment aimlessly would only amp up my anxiety. A little fresh air wouldn't hurt and it gave me an excuse to get in my first caffeinated beverage of the day. As I walked these familiar streets, my mind wandered back to Kevin. *Did he find the help he needed? Would he still reach out to the magical community or would he continue to suffer in silence?*

Pushing those thoughts aside, I tried to focus on what waited ahead of me. I only knew one FBI agent in Boston—two if you counted the bastard who'd used and abused Kevin—but we barely knew each other. There was no way the call for me to head back here came from her. We'd only crossed paths a couple of times back when Ezri was dismantling the Order.

Without realizing it, my feet had carried me far past my coffee destination and I now stood at the outer entrance to a cemetery. I knew it wasn't open for visiting hours. Though as I stood there, a gust of wind rushed past me and I could swear I heard a familiar voice urging me onward. I glanced skyward checking for cameras. There didn't' appear to be any surveillance here which meant I wouldn't simply disappear from footage. That was good. I didn't need to raise unnecessary questions.

Dropping my guard was easy. I blew out a breath and my magic rose up around me like a blanket I'd almost forgotten wearing. It draped itself around me, filling my nose with lavender. The air around me shimmered as the intent of my spell took form. I didn't even need to think it very hard. This was the thing I most frequently asked of my magic. It was basically on autopilot. My body turned invisible starting at the tips of my fingers, radiating upward and outward in a fractal pattern until I was no longer visible. The gate's bars were too close together for me to slip through and I wasn't' wearing the right kind of shoes to scale it.

"Time to get creative," I sighed and wrapped my hands around the bars.

Power rushed from my core into my hands as I willed the bars to disappear for just a few seconds. Long enough for me to get through. When I opened my eyes again, the bars had vanished and I stepped through. They reappeared the moment my body lost contact with the metal.

It didn't take me long to realize where I was meant to go. The faint traces of berries and mint drew me to a pair of headstones. Ones I hadn't visited before. A wave of guilt washed over me as I stood there looking down at where two of the bravest people I'd ever known were laid to rest. Both graves had fresh flowers laid on them and the area around the heavy stones was well-maintained. Some of that likely came down to the groundskeeping staff employed by the cemetery. But I wouldn't put it past their family to add a little extra boost of magic to keep the place looking respectable.

"Hey," I said, offering the air a small wave. "So, I know it's been well, forever and I haven't been to see you guys. Sorry about that."

I shoved my hands into my pockets. "I think you'd both be proud of me. I went back to school, got my degree in criminology. Just graduated top of my class at Quantico. So, I've finally made something of myself."

The breeze blew by again, and I swore I heard voices whispering, "We're proud of you." Logically, I knew it had to be a trick my brain was playing, but I took it for the ego boost I needed it to be.

"I start my first assignment as an agent today. I'm kind of nervous about the whole thing if I'm being honest. I mean, Des, you know my baggage. You know how much I don't like being the center of attention."

Another wave of emotion crashed into me, knocking me back a step. It had been waiting to strike since yesterday. When I'd told Kevin he should talk to someone, I'd been so wrapped up in the fact he was dumping me I couldn't put names to the feeling—grief and sadness. Not at the loss of the relationship, not really. There was too much hurt and anger still simmering on the surface for me to feel those deeper emotions. No, my grief stemmed from a relationship that had ended two years ago.

"You know, Des, I think I'm still mad at you for getting yourself killed. You were always there for me. Just to listen. I could use that now and so could Kevin. He's out of prison. I know he hasn't dealt with the loss of his magic. You'd be the perfect person to help him through that."

Standing in the silence, I let out a soft sob and tears trickled down my cheeks. I'd been holding onto that heartbreak for far too long.

As I caught my breath, I felt a tiny weight lift from my chest.

I pivoted, looking now at Ezri's headstone. We hadn't exactly been friends, not in the traditional sense. But I knew she'd relied on me and I helped save lives. That counted in her book. "You inspired me you know? Before I met you, I never would have given this whole law enforcement thing a chance. You made me realize that I didn't have to let my magic define me. Even though you knew you were marching toward a destiny you probably wouldn't walk away from, you still did everything you could to help people along the way." I dabbed at my cheeks. "You know, I regret a lot of things in my life, but knowing you isn't one of them."

My phone beeped in my pocket and I checked the display. I now had half an hour before I would be late for my first day. "I promise, now that I'm back home for a little while, I'll come visit more."

I retraced my steps and with a little effort, slipped back through the gate. I held onto my invisibility long enough to ensure I didn't get caught on any other cameras that might be in the area. When the magic dropped away, it was like I could breathe again. I'd spent so much time thinking I had no choice but to let my magic control me, that being in the driver's seat still felt weird. Just another thing Desmond would have helped me with if he'd been around and that made me sad all over again.

I had just enough time to grab my coffee, but not drink it before arriving downtown at FBI headquarters. The security guards gave me side-eye as I stepped up and held out my credentials. Though they waved me through, ignoring the loud blaring as my guns set off the metal detector. I stopped short at the elevator bank, realizing I had no idea where I was supposed to go beyond that.

"Agent Rogers." I turned to see Agent Duncan striding toward me. He looked like he hadn't slept much.

"Either you're following me or you pulled

the short straw in escorting the new girl around," I said, but gave him a grateful smile.

"Maybe a little of both?" His cheeks burned bright as his words hung in the air between us.

I didn't like the thought of a stranger following me around, especially one without any magic. Except I also couldn't deny he had a certain dorky charm to him. *That's just your rebound reflex.*

He cleared his throat and hit the 'Up' button on the elevator bank. We stood side-by-side until one arrived, announcing its presence with a loud 'ding.' He held his arm out to keep the door from closing, letting me get on first. I watched as he scanned his credentials by the row of buttons before hitting the button for the fifth floor. I committed that sequence to memory. I didn't need him to get me every day.

"So, how long have you been an agent?" I filled the dead air between us as the elevator's hydraulics whirred above us.

"Six months."

Another relative newbie, interesting.

"We must have just missed each other at the academy then," I said.

"Yeah, must have. Though I doubt I'd forget meeting you," he said. That deep blush returned to his cheeks. I could imagine the conversation in his head, chiding himself for his poor attempts at flirting. Since I had to believe even he knew how cringe-worthy that sounded, I let out a nervous hiccup of laughter that seemed to ease the tension between us.

"I think you're really going to like the team," he said, drumming his fingers on the side of his leg, casting his gaze up to the numbers as they scrolled by.

Before I could pepper him with questions about whether he'd chosen this assignment or if he had some unknown skillset that made him a high-value team asset, we reached our destination and the doors slid open. He stepped out first this time and I fell into step beside him. We turned left down a short hallway to a door marked 'Room 512.' He tapped his credentials again to get into the room. Another mental note taken that I'd need to use them for entry without an escort.

The space was filled with cubicles. Row upon row of prefabricated dividers sectioned off desks. The first thing I noticed was the silence. He led me back through the rows of cramped spaces with their not-in-use computers and chairs. If this was supposed to be a taskforce, where were the other people? Duncan stopped at the door to what I guessed was a conference room. It had floor to ceiling windows with the shades drawn. Still, I caught hints of movement from within and I could pick up on the low murmur of voices. It was too soft to discern actual words. Duncan didn't open the door or otherwise indicate we should go in. He just stood there glancing from the door to me and back again. He opened his mouth a time or two, but didn't speak. The alarm I'd set on my phone to make sure I wasn't late went off, filling the space with an obnoxious little jig I didn't remember picking. It was probably the preprogramed default on the phone. I scrambled to turn it off. I could feel his eyes on me as I slammed my finger on the screen, desperately trying to make the stupid thing stop. Embarrassment flushed my cheeks and I knew if I looked down, the spot just above my collarbone would be pink. Like I'd gotten an odd sunburn.

The sound drew the attention of the occupants inside the conference room. The conversation died instantly, and the movement ceased, too. Except no one came to see who had forgotten to set their phone to silent before entering the building. So, either they weren't that curious or it wasn't that unusual of an occurrence. Duncan kept trying to cover an amused smile, but it was like his mouth had a mind of its own and it needed me to know it understood my embarrassment.

"Aren't we supposed to go in?" I prodded, praying it would diffuse the tension brewing around us.

His phone beeped and he retrieved it from the interior pocket of his suit jacket. He glanced at the screen before looking back at me. "Uh, just you."

If he was trying to be reassuring, he had failed. *Epically*. I didn't like not knowing what I was walking into, but I wasn't going to let him see me sweat. I swallowed the fear rising in my throat and pushed past him to the door. My hand waivered above the handle and for a split second the tips of my fingers vanished. I turned my body enough to hide the errant magic as I willed my hand back into being. Thankfully, he didn't seem to notice. I pressed down on the handle and the door swung inward to reveal a long table with chairs scattered around it. Immediately to my right I spotted a mess of images and details on a white board that made little sense to me. At the far end of the table, two female figures huddled with their backs turned to me.

"Excuse me," I said, hoping I didn't sound as nervous as I suddenly felt.

Slowly, the taller of the two turned to face me and my jaw went slack. Detective Jacquie DeWitt, Ezri's partner on the police force stood there looking at me with her intense dark eyes and no-nonsense expression. As I tried to form words, my brain computed the information. If there was a taskforce, of course she'd be on it. She was with the police. Except, she, too, wore FBI credentials and a badge clipped to them. And then the second figure spun to reveal Agent Molly Cartwright. Her blonde hair was longer than the last time I'd seen her, but she was otherwise unchanged.

"Glad you could join us, Agent Rogers," she said. "Now, close the door. We need to talk."

FOUR

Blood rushed in my ears as I stared at the two familiar faces at the other end of the table. It took a few extra seconds for her words to register in my brain and I tried to cover my awkward pause with a cough before stepping back to ease the door shut. Agent Duncan still stood there, and I gave him what I hoped passed for an apologetic smile.

Pivoting back to face the table, I gripped the chair in front of me. "Uh, I have questions." The words tumbled out of my mouth before I could stop them. Definitely not the move of a professional.

Agent Cartwright gave me a broad grin and gestured for me to take a seat. "We figured you might."

She sat down and I followed suit. Detective—no, Agent—DeWitt remained standing. She still had that tough-as-nails expression and stance that challenged anyone approaching her to think twice.

"So, who goes first?" My voice caught in my throat.

"Ask your questions," Agent DeWitt answered.

"I'm assuming I have at least one of you to thank for this last-minute assignment?"

"That would be correct," Agent DeWitt replied.

"We have to keep an eye on the rising talent coming out of Quantico and figured having you on our radar was the least we could do," Agent Cartwright added.

Her words carried an unspoken subtext— Ezri would have wanted them to have my back. Our relationship had been anything but conventional and far too brief. Yet I couldn't help thinking how much she'd touched our lives.

"I appreciate you looking out for me, but I wasn't exactly planning to come back. At least not right away," I admitted.

"The world has a way of working things out the way they need to happen. If I've learned anything working cases with you all, it's that sometimes you don't question the universe. You just go with it," Agent Cartwright offered.

I eyed Agent DeWitt. "You left the department?"

She touched the badge hanging around her neck. It was an almost subconscious gesture. "You weren't the only one who needed a change after everything that went down with the Order."

Neither woman across the table from me had magic. Despite that, they were as wrapped up in the supernatural world as I was. They had both seen first-hand what the Order of Samael could do. But Ezri had dismantled their organization before she'd sacrificed herself. *Hadn't she?*

"I understand that," I murmured. "I guess she inspired a lot of us to make big changes."

Agent Cartwright ducked her head and studied her hands, her fingers splayed against the faux wood tabletop. "And some of us are just trying to carry on her legacy of protecting those who can't protect themselves. Even ..."

"Even without magic," I filled in for her.

I hadn't spent a lot of time around the Authority's headquarters since I'd gone back to school and entered Quantico. Though I had expected to see Agent DeWitt around more, given what had happened to her niece, Neveah.

"How's your niece?" I tried to make eye contact, so she could see that I was genuinely interested in the girl's wellbeing. She'd been through hell at the hands of the Order.

"She's getting there. Some days are harder than others." Her expression didn't betray any emotion.

"I can imagine." I knew Desmond had been helping her before he'd been killed. So many of the people who'd put me on this journey had their lives cut short. It wasn't fair. "I'm sorry she lost her support."

"We all lost him," she reminded me softly.

"We lost them both," I breathed.

I wanted to tell them about my trip to the cemetery and the awkward break-up with Kevin. Except those felt like things I would share with friends and no matter what shared experiences I had with these two women; we weren't friends. They were still outsiders in my world. They may have connections to the magical world by virtue of their connection to Ezri, but neither of them had magic.

"As much as I'm sure we'd like to keep going down memory lane, if you've gotten your questions out of the way, I would like to explain why you're here," Agent Cartwright said, drumming her fingers on the table.

I cleared my throat and a moment of panic flared as my right hand turned translucent. Lavender flooded my nose and I had to tamp down on my magic. Hard. It lasted only a few seconds and when I looked over at the other agents, I wasn't sure they'd even noticed the slip-up.

Just another time I wished Desmond had still been here to ground me—to offer some supportive word of comfort or wisdom to get my head on straight. Only he was gone, and I was still here. I hated to admit that I still felt so lost without him. It had been nearly two years and I was still pissed at both him and Ezri. I hadn't gotten to say goodbye to either of them.

"Right, sorry. What's going on? All I know is that you requested me specifically for a taskforce."

My ears pricked up at the sound of shuffling feet in the cubicle farm beyond our conference room. Had Agent Duncan been listening in on our conversation? I probably should have asked whether we could speak openly around him, but had been so caught off guard it had slipped my mind.

Agent DeWitt made a swirling motion and pointed to the whiteboard behind me. I pivoted to look at the collection of information. It still meant nothing to me, but I waited patiently for one of them to explain the details. Hoping my role would become clear soon enough.

"Before we get into the nitty gritty, we should let you know that we are aware of your history," Agent DeWitt said.

Heat flashed down my neck and I bowed my head. I'd made a lot of mistakes when my magic turned on me. "It didn't stop me from entering the academy," I murmured.

"I'm sure your particular brand of magic had a hand in making sure you weren't caught," Agent Cartwright added.

She'd experienced my magic first-hand when I'd snuck her and Ezri into the hospital during a case. The same one that had nearly broken Neveah. "Ezri knew about it, too," I said. "It's how she knew to ask me about Lola Cox." Lola had been manipulated by the Order into abducting children. She wasn't like that when we'd first met. She'd died for her affiliations.

"We all have things in our pasts we aren't proud of. The point is, your past is uniquely relevant to this case," Agent Cartwright continued. The chair she'd been occupying squeaked as she rose and moved to stand in my field of vision by the whiteboard.

I let her words sink in. Something about my past was important to a case. That didn't seem right. I'd been out of that life for a long time and had worked hard to distance myself. I'd been uncomfortable even sharing what I knew about Lola with Ezri years ago. "What are you talking about?"

"We've been following a series of bank robberies across the city." Agent Cartwright tapped several red pins on a map of downtown Boston. I studied their placement, but didn't see anything that would signal a pattern.

"And you think, because I used to … dabble I'd have some insight?" I asked.

"It's more than that. The method these people are using has the rest of the agency and local officers stumped," she continued. "They go in with one or two people who keep the tellers' attention and then safety deposit boxes are broken into."

"But there's no surveillance to show how they're getting into the buildings," Agent DeWitt offered from her position at the far end of the conference table.

"And you think they're using magic," I surmised.

"Not just any magic, Whisperer magic."

It made a certain amount of sense. I'd never fully understood why my magic worked the way it did. Though it not only allowed me to turn my entire body invisible to both the naked eye and surveillance equipment, but I could alter the density of my body. Like I'd done at the cemetery.

"Because there aren't any other alarms tripped," I said.

"Exactly."

I stood and stepped up to the map, studying the addresses again. "Has anyone been hurt? Are they taking hostages?"

"So far there've been minor injuries and by

the time police response arrives, the thieves are gone," Agent Cartwright answered.

"They're polite. Chat up the tellers. They haven't needed to make threats," Agent DeWitt added.

That tickled something in the back of my mind, but I couldn't quite put my finger on it. At least we knew for the moment they weren't violent. "What's been taken from the safety deposit boxes?"

"That's the thing, usually nothing. Maybe some cash if it's in there. We haven't figured out what they're looking for. But they've hit six banks in two months." Agent Cartwright tapped two spots on the map. "The last two were only a week apart."

"They're escalating," I murmured.

"We think they've had lookouts to let them know when the police are getting close," Agent DeWitt said.

"Do the ones who go into the bank have masks? Are they obscuring their identities?" I asked, trying to fit the pieces together.

"They never face the cameras and none of

the eyewitnesses can give an accurate facial sketch." I caught the frustration in her tone.

"You think they're using magic to tamper with memory."

"It's a possibility," Agent Cartwright noted. "We think we've got a lead on one of their lookouts." She pointed to a mug shot of a girl who couldn't have been older than fourteen or fifteen. "Sylvia Lawrence. She's got a few charges on her rap sheet for petty stuff."

The name didn't ring any bells, but not every person and family in the Commonwealth worked with the Authority. Most people were aware of its existence and the protection it could offer, but some people didn't like the idea of being part of a system like that. There were hundreds of people out there learning magic on their own. "She's not going to turn. Whoever she's working for, she's likely getting a place to stay and food. They're giving her things she needs."

"Where would you start?" Agent DeWitt's question made me jump. Not because of the substance, but because I hadn't noticed her move to stand on my other side.

"You aren't going to find much, especially if they don't want to be found. But I'd want to know what they're looking for. They clearly think it's something valuable."

"The safety deposit boxes all have the same number," Agent Duncan's voice made the three of us turn in unison.

His cheeks flushed. "Sorry, I just ... I heard you talking about the banks and realized that all the safety deposit boxes had the same number. I've got a memory for numbers."

He handed me a case file and I studied the contents. Each image was labeled with a bank name, address, and date. The contents of each box appeared disturbed, but mostly there. They ranged from gold and jewelry to documents. But each one clearly had the same number, 664.

He was right. This was definitely important. "Is there any other connection between who the boxes belong to?"

He shook his head. "Not that we've been able to figure out yet."

"Do we have any idea how many other banks in the city have safety deposit boxes that go up this high?"

His eyes lit up and he took the file back. "Not yet, but give me a little time and we will."

I turned to the map, trying to look at the locations of the banks with fresh eyes. I held out my hand and made a grasping motion for the file he'd taken. He handed it back and I glanced through the dates again, making a mental note of the sequence on the map. "Does it look like they started at the outskirts of the city and have been working their way toward downtown?"

"You weren't kidding when you said she'd be an asset to the team," Duncan praised.

Agent Cartwright tilted her head to one side and traced the red pins on the map with the tip of her index finger. "You might be right."

"The sooner we know how many more banks in the area have safety deposit boxes, the sooner we can determine where they might hit next," I said.

Duncan took the file back a second time and stood there in the doorway, looking eager to hear more. If we wanted to find anything about who was behind this, I knew where I needed to start and I had no desire to go there. That was far too close to dredging up the past, especially with the questions I would need to ask. There was no way I was going to say it with Agent Duncan in earshot. Besides, I wasn't about to tell him where he could or couldn't be, this wasn't my investigation.

"So, how would you go about tracking these guys down?" Agent Cartwright asked again.

"I would try to figure out where they might be hanging out, recruiting their other lookouts. If they're dipping into the juvenile offender pool, there are only a few places I would go." I turned to Agent Cartwright and lowered my voice. "I might have an idea of where to start, but I'm going to need some discreet backup."

She nodded in silent understanding. Time for an awkward trip down memory lane.

FIVE

I hadn't been back to Notre Dame in nearly two years. It was one of the only bars in the city that catered specifically to magical clientele. It was one of those open secrets. Sure, it attracted some mundane college kids too, but they just attributed the strange happenings to the alcohol.

We were going early enough in the day that there shouldn't be any patrons. That meant there was zero chance of me blending in with the crowd. But that was the point, wasn't it? I wanted to be seen.

"You sure you're okay doing this?" Agent

DeWitt asked, falling into step beside me as we approached the bar.

"I don't think we have much choice," I answered.

Agent Cartwright—I really had a hard time thinking of them as people without using first names—stepped in front of me to bar my way forward. "Before we get in there, we should clear the air. You've got some history with the owner?"

I guess Ezri had filled them in a little. "Back when I was on the … uh wrong side of the law, we sometimes operated out of the bar. And on occasion we'd run some errands for him. Nothing big-time."

"And he was pissed when you got out of the life?" she pressed.

"You'd have to ask him. I stopped coming around after I got on the straight and narrow with the Authority. I didn't need that temptation."

"You two seemed to do fine at Ezri's wake," she noted.

I let out a bitter laugh "Because there were

other people for him to pay attention to. It wasn't one-on-one."

"Which is why we're here," Agent DeWitt added, patting me on the shoulder.

I nodded and cleared my throat. "There's one other thing before we go in. Uh, I know I'm just right out of the academy and everything. You're obviously my superiors, but is it okay if …" I trailed off, embarrassment turning my neck warm.

"Call us by our first names? Definitely," Molly said with a smile.

"I'd prefer it," Jacquie added.

Relief washed over me and I let out an audible sigh. "Thanks."

With that awkwardness behind us, I led the way to the bar. The usual security was absent. Then again, I suppose it didn't make sense to pay for a bouncer when there weren't patrons on the premises. I pulled open the front door and marched in. It felt strange coming back here on official business. A part of me wondered if Jonathan would be impressed with where I'd gone in my life. Or would I always be the low-level wannabe criminal he'd used for his own purposes.

"We're not open," a gruff voice called from behind the bar.

Time to find out. I held up my badge and replied, "I think you'll want to make an exception."

My voice bounced around the empty space, feeling foreign to my own ears. It was enough to draw his attention. Jonathan pivoted to face us and I was reminded just how disarming his appearance could be. Not because I knew he was using magic to hide a physical deformity, but because his face was so strikingly handsome. The façade he wore only enhanced that attractiveness.

His gaze narrowed and settled on me before moving to my companions. "Somebody got an upgrade."

"I see you're still slinging beer," I replied.

"Do what you know," he answered, leaning both elbows on the bar. He turned his attention to Molly. "What have I done this time to incur the FBI's presence in my bar?"

The way he spoke made me wonder if there were other cases she and Jacquie had worked in the last two years that used Jonathan as a source. Or if he was referring to one of the times she and Ezri had worked cases together.

"That remains to be seen," Molly answered coolly.

"We all know you have a tendency to attract the less law-abiding segments of the magical community," I interjected.

"You'd know, wouldn't you?" he quipped.

I knew he was trying to get under my skin and rattle me. He knew all of my insecurities and what buttons to push, but I wasn't going to let him get the better of me. I was stronger than the girl I'd been when we were in each other's orbits years ago. I'd grown and he was still standing in the same place, running the same bar.

"Not that this isn't amusing, but we have a job to do," Jacquie said, stepping up to the bar.

Jonathan turned his attention to her. "You

always were the no-nonsense one," he commented.

She made a show of looking around the vacant bar. "If the next words out of your mouth are going to disparage my former partner, I would seriously think twice. You may have magic, but you aren't the only one who can pack a punch."

He held up his hands in a defensive posture. "I never speak ill of the dead." A mask of sadness passed over his features for a moment. He really had been fond of Ezri. "Just tell me what you want."

Time to prove to him just how much I'd changed. "We're looking for a bank heist crew."

He laughed. "You ought to be talking to your own, ladies."

"We both know I've been out of the scene for a long time," I ground out. "Have you heard anyone around bragging about hitting banks?"

"You seem to think they all just blab about their exploits. These people aren't idiots," he scoffed. "They have a code and know when to keep their mouths shut."

"Come on, you know everything that happens in this bar. You've always heard things other people wouldn't," I prodded.

He leaned closer and I tried not to look away from the intensity of his gaze. "And people tell me things, because they trust me."

"You've helped law enforcement before," Molly offered.

"People who hurt kids are the exception," he said.

"Just because no one's been hurt yet, doesn't mean they won't. Whoever this crew is they're escalating. And they aren't stopping until they find what they're looking for," I said, irritation coloring my voice.

"Then I guess you'd better go investigate, *Agent*," he answered.

Before I could respond, Molly slipped him her card. "If those ears of yours happen to pick up on anything, call me."

He bristled, but took the card. I barely contained my temper as we left the bar behind. I should have known he wouldn't tell me anything. He was still pissed at me. I stalked up and down the stretch of sidewalk beside the bar and took deep breaths. Getting angry wasn't going to do any good and I could feel my magic rising to the surface, itching to just hide me away from the world while I raged.

"I know that look," Jacquie said calmly, catching my eye. "You're beating yourself up, because your lead didn't pan out. Don't go down that road."

"It's that obvious?" I groaned.

"You've been on this case for all of a few hours. We weren't expecting miracles," she replied.

"I don't know where we go from here," I sighed.

"We keep digging into the safety deposit box number angle," Molly answered.

It was a logical avenue to follow and my instincts told me it was the right move, but there was more to the magic in this case. I felt it.

# UNSEEN MAGIC

"I'm going to pay a visit to some other old acquaintances and see if they've heard anything," I offered.

"We'll call you as soon as we hear from Agent Duncan," Molly said.

She and Jacquie left me standing on the sidewalk and for a minute I stayed rooted to the spot in surprise. I was a new field agent with zero experience. Yet, they were letting me run off on my own. A tiny voice in the back of my head warned that this felt like a setup, like they were hoping I'd fail. Except that was my own self-doubt creeping in. They'd requested me out of any other agent they could have and they needed me. Now I just had to prove them right.

LIKE MUCH OF BOSTON, returning to the Authority headquarters felt surreal. It had been my safe space since I'd met Desmond and he brought me into the fold. It still felt like home, more than my own ever had. Only it had continued growing and changing in my absence. There were too many new faces I didn't recognize.

I pulled into the circular drive and headed inside. Luckily, the change in leadership had not changed the interior layout of the building. It still had the large library off to one side, the kitchen in the far back, and the main meeting room up on the second floor, accessible by a winding staircase. The one new addition that hadn't been present the last time I'd been here was a tastefully hung portrait and plaque of Ezri leading into the library. I studied it, noting it listed her name, date of death, and the words *'Her sacrifice lives on in each of us.'*

"She'd hate it," a familiar voice said from behind me.

I turned to find Avery Fellowes standing there. Her trademark headphones still sat around her neck. Her glasses were smaller these days. She was much more a resigned widow trying to carry on than the bubbly, edgy tech whiz she'd been before.

I found myself smiling in spite of myself. "Yeah, she would," I agreed.

"I didn't know you were back in town," Avery said and gestured for me to follow her into the kitchen.

It was an industrial space with a long table and stainless-steel appliances. It felt far more modern than the rest of the place. I could feel the presence of magic all around me, but it didn't call to my power. It was more like the building had developed its own magical signature over the years composed of a piece of every practitioner who'd come through it.

"I only got back yesterday," I said. We weren't the best of friends, but our grief over our shared loss had bonded us. Yet, I hadn't thought to let her know I was back in Boston.

She gestured to the badge hanging around my neck. "I see they actually let you through."

"Graduated top of my class," I beamed. "How have things been around here?"

She fiddled with the electric kettle on the stove. "Quiet. Too quiet if you ask me."

Her words caught my attention. "How so?"

The kettle clicked to life and began boiling water someone had already poured in. "I don't know exactly. Maybe it's just in my head, but it always felt like there was a lot going on you know … before …"

She didn't need to finish her thought for me to know what she meant. The year that Ezri returned to the fold had seen more activity in this place than there had been in decades. "We're all just trying to live up to their legacy," I said.

"I know, but it's hard. I'm a police widow, but I don't really belong there. Everyone I knew there is gone."

"They're still around. We all are," I said, offering her a sympathetic look.

"The FBI doesn't need me. They've got their own people who are far better trained than the police."

"For mundane crimes, maybe. But you're still the best magical tech genius I've ever met." Subconsciously I knew that was why I'd come here in the first place. I'd hoped she would be here and would agree to help.

"You don't honestly need my help," she said as the kettle whistled.

"Actually, I do. We're working a case ... a bank heist crew and we could use your help reviewing the footage."

Her eyes widened within the frames of her glasses. "If you really think I can help, I'll take a look."

"Great. I'll get copies of the footage sent over."

"What are they after?" she prodded.

"We're not sure yet," I answered. Even though she was on our side, I didn't want to divulge too much information early. I accepted the mug of tea she offered me as I tried to plan my next move. We knew the crew hadn't found what they were looking for yet, so they were bound to hit more banks in the city. We knew they were using at least one Whisperer to get into the safety deposit boxes unseen.

While another member of the crew kept lookout and a third occupied the tellers.

"Kayla?" Avery's voice drew me out of my thoughts.

I shook my head. "Sorry, just trying to figure out where to go next. This is my first case."

"I know she didn't show it much, but she'd be proud of you."

I nodded and clutched the tea mug between my hands. "I know. They both would. I have to admit though, this is one of those times where I really wish I had Desmond to talk to."

She bowed her head at the mention of her husband. "I can't even pretend to know what he'd say to you."

"Probably something about how I have it within me to do this."

"Sometimes I really hate prophecies," Avery murmured.

So, did I. It didn't seem fair that one family should have to endure so much loss, so the rest of us could live in peace and safety. Also

I'd never understand how they both had faced what waited for them with such poise and dignity. I would have been a mess—kicking and screaming, and looking for any loophole I could to break free. But maybe that's why they were the heroes.

Before I could say anything else, my phone buzzed in my pocket. I pulled it out to see an unfamiliar number flashing on the screen. "Agent Rogers."

"Kayla? Honey?" My mother's voice sounded unsure on the other end of the line.

I hadn't given my parents the number for the phone I'd gotten for work. "Why are you calling me?" I turned my back on Avery and set the mug down on the counter to avoid dropping it.

"I wanted to see you. We need to talk."

"I'm working." How dare she horn in on my life now when she'd been happy to pretend I no longer existed for years.

"It will only take a few minutes. Please, can we meet in the tea garden at the library?"

I picked up on the fear in her voice. Something was wrong. For someone whose paranoia had fueled my own magic turning on me, for her to be afraid of something meant it couldn't be ignored.

"I'll be there in half an hour."

SIX

The sense of dread settling in the pit of my stomach should have been all the warning I needed to know this meeting with my mother would end poorly. The space was sparsely populated at this time of day and I grabbed a table in a corner with my back facing the exterior wall. It gave me a good vantage point to spot her coming and an easy means of escape if I needed to ghost her.

The thought of running chilled me to my core. Those were the instincts of a girl on the run, trying to avoid getting caught.

You're not her anymore.

As I sat there waiting for my mother to show up, I couldn't help going over the highlights of my misspent youth. My magic had turned against me in college, not long after Kevin had 'disappeared' from my life. I hadn't thought about it much at the time, but what the Order of Samael had done to him was the starting point of my life changing. In a way, him coming back into my life when Ezri found him had jumpstarted another change.

The thoughts of Kevin brought tears to my eyes and I blinked them away. Whatever my mom was coming to tell me, she couldn't see me cry. I knew her. She'd take advantage of my emotions and twist them to fit her own ends.

The interior doors to the tea garden opened and I pivoted to track the movement. I almost didn't recognize my mom. Her hair had gone a dark grey and she had more bags under her eyes. Her skin was sallow and drawn. Her hands fidgeted with the clasp of her bag as she scanned the tables until our gazes met. She hurried over and sat down.

"You're really here," she murmured, the disbelief in her tone making my own chest hurt.

"I told you I would," I answered. "But whatever you have to say, just tell me. I don't have time to waste here."

Her slender fingers flexed and tightened around the strap of her bag sitting on the table between us. "I heard you were back in town and I wanted to tell you … I'm sorry."

I gaped at her. Those were not the words I'd ever expected to hear from her. "For what?" I croaked.

"Everything. For pushing you away, for not being around when you were growing up."

"You do realize that the way you treated me literally changed my magic," I hissed. This wasn't the place to have this kind of conversation, but there was no other choice. I'd opened my mouth and my voice would be silent no longer. "The way you raised me, affected me to the point where my magic made me *invisible*."

"I know." Mom wouldn't look me in the eye now. "I understand more than you know."

As if on cue, her hands turned translucent. She tried to hide them as the effect spread up to her elbows. Her lips quivered and what little color had been in her cheeks faded. I could feel more than see the effort of her will, trying to regain control of her power.

"You expect me to be sympathetic?" I snapped.

"I wanted to tell you that I now understand what you went through and I truly am sorry for what I did to you. I fought it for so long."

I had to ball my hands into tight fists to keep my own magic in check. The scent of lavender rose up around me, wanting to hide me away from the discomfort of this conversation. "Fought what? Being a lousy mother? If you think the fact that your magic turned on you is going to fix years of distrust and pain, you're delusional."

"No, Kayla. I'm sick. I think a part of me knew it for a while, but I didn't want to admit it. I thought maybe I could ignore it and it would go away. But I was wrong."

"Sick? Like what, cancer or something?'

"No, honey." One hand solidified itself and she tapped at her temple. "Up here."

I sat back in my chair, putting as much distance as I could between us. Yet again I wished Desmond was around to help me sort through this. He could have told me if what she said was true. If she had some undiagnosed condition that had made her paranoid. The fleeting worry that whatever had manifested in her would appear in me soured my stomach.

"Look, I'm glad you're getting help for whatever you think is wrong with you. I'm sorry you have to deal with becoming a Whisperer, but I can't help you. I spent so much of my life wanting to please you and realizing I couldn't, was the best thing I ever did for myself."

I didn't want to be in this space anymore, to sit here listening to my mother try to apologize for years of trauma. I could fake an incoming call for work. She'd never know the difference. My hand slipped beneath the table and into my pocket when she reached across the table for my free hand.

"This isn't the only reason I wanted to see you." Her head turned first to the right and then to the left as if to ensure we weren't being spied on. "I'm trying to learn how these new powers work. And the people I found … I don't know if I can trust them. And I don't know if that's just in my head or if it's real."

"What people?" My fingers brushed the edge of my phone and stopped. The Whisperer community wasn't big. I might not know all the current players, but some names stuck in my memory as ones to avoid. I could at least point her in the right direction.

"They said that they would help, but that I needed to do something for them first."

I don't like the sound of that.

"What sort of things, Mom?"

"I just have to show up and stand on a corner. I mean it seems almost silly. Like hazing or something."

Or a way to make sure that a robbery crew wasn't caught. If they're switching lookouts on each job, that made the FBI's job that much more difficult. If they were recruiting new Whisperers who didn't' know the ropes, they were expendable, too. They wouldn't need to know any more than where to be. They wouldn't know what was really going on.

"This is really important, Mom. Where did you meet these people?"

"I don't remember. Around." She gave a vague hand wave to accentuate her point.

"Not good enough," I snapped. "I need to know where they got in touch with you."

"So, it's something I should be worried about?" she prodded.

"If it's what I think it is, yes. And if you go along with them, you're going to end up in jail."

"What are you talking about?'

"They're criminals, Mom," I answered.

"You may think it sounds stupid to stand on a corner, but they are using you to get what they want. You better believe the first chance they get; you'll be tossed under the bus."

Her gaze narrowed. There was that trademark suspicion I'd come to expect with my mother. "How do you know all of this?"

"Because I'm hunting them down." I slammed my FBI badge on the table between us. "Or did you forget I now work for the FBI?"

The distrust went out of her eyes, replaced by fear. I could guess at the flurry of questions running through her mind right now. Would I turn her in, because she simply talked to people engaged in criminal activity? Could she still trust me at all, because I was now part of 'the establishment?'

"Look, if you tell me where you met them, we're even. Whatever happened between us is in the past," I offered.

"I don't want that Kayla. I want to know my daughter. I want to work through things in my life with you there. I want to fix what I broke the best I'm able."

And what about what I want?

"I'm not sure I'm ready to let you back into my life, Mom," I said bluntly.

"I can try to be patient," she offered. "I don't want to lose you again."

"Then *help* me."

I hated having to beg her for anything. She should want to help me catch criminals. There was a part of me that wondered if she'd been disappointed in my life choices, because she was so worried about the police showing up on her doorstep. Or had she pretended she didn't know anything about what I'd been up to when Lola had taken me under her wing? It pained me to think that Lola might have actually been able to help me if she weren't dead. Then again, maybe that wasn't as big an impediment as it could be. Another possible thread to chase down later.

"Was it a bar?" I prodded. I knew feeding her too much information might make her agree with me just so she could seem useful. I didn't need to chase my tail if she lied to me.

"No. I don't think so."

"So, the name Notre Dame doesn't ring any bells?"

She shook her head. "It was just like … oh why can't I remember?"

I wasn't convinced this wasn't just an act she was putting on to test me. She rubbed at her temples.. "The doctor gave me medication and it makes things fuzzy sometimes."

"Do you remember what the people looked like? Any landmarks? Anything I can use?"

"No. It's all just so fuzzy. But it might come back to me if I just skip a pill or two."

"No, Mom. If you're supposed to be taking meds, take them."

"What if I could find them again and went along with what they asked? I could just give you the information," she said, her eyes starting to brighten. "It would let me see what your life is like now."

"No. Absolutely not. You're not going undercover. For one thing, having a family member involved would never fly with my superiors. And for another, you wouldn't even know what you're doing. Besides, if you're memory is that impaired by your meds, then you wouldn't be a reliable witness if things went to trial."

"I happen to have more skills than you think," she scoffed. "Just because I'm new to these powers doesn't mean I don't' know how to use magic, Kayla."

"The answer is still no," I replied. I couldn't believe she was trying to insert herself into my life like this.

I wasn't going to get anything else from her. I'd have better luck heading back to FBI headquarters to see if Jacquie and Molly had found anything more on the safety deposit box numbers. I needed to get the video footage sent over to Avery, too. Though maybe this visit hadn't been a total waste. At least now I knew how the crew was recruiting their lookouts. If I could find where they were recruiting from, I could use that to my advantage.

"I can't say that this has been helpful or even pleasant, Mom," I said and stood up. "But I need to go. I have a case to solve."

Stepping around the table, I started for the exit. Her hand wrapped around my wrist. I could so easily turn it insubstantial and flee her grip. I could use the way my magic worked, thanks to her, against her. Only that would be pushing me closer to the girl I'd been back then. When I'd used my magic for my own ends? I wasn't that person anymore.

"Kayla, wait," Mom called, tugging on my wrist so that I had no other choice, but to turn back to look at her. "I think I remember a name. Ragland. I think it was a last name."

The name didn't ring any bells, but that didn't mean anything. I hadn't known all of the players back in the day. It had been safer to only associate with the people I'd trusted. The fewer people who knew the details of our activity, the less chance we had of getting caught. That probably held true for this Ragland person, too. Besides, I had more resources at my disposal now than I had even just a few short weeks ago. "Thank you."

I pulled my hand free, secured my badge in my pocket, and left the garden behind. The sun had started its afternoon descent toward the horizon. There would still be hours of daylight left, but weariness settled over me. I'd been hitting dead ends all day and I needed a win. As I started down Boylston Street in the direction of the Boston Common, my phone buzzed in my pocket. Tugging it from my pocket I checked the display to see an unfamiliar number identified as 'Maybe Duncan.' I really should put his number in the contacts just to be safe.

"This is Agent Rogers," I answered.

"I hope I haven't caught you at a bad time." Agent Duncan's voice came through from the other end of the call.

"Perfect timing, actually." I couldn't hide the smile that had appeared on my lips. I cleared my throat and added, "Did you find anything with the safety deposit numbers?"

"Not yet. I was just wondering if you wanted anything for dinner."

The unsure cadence of his words had my hackles up. He'd been terrible at flirting when we'd first met. Was this another weak attempt? Or was he after something else? Either way, I could use something to eat and I had already been on my way back to headquarters.

"Is this a common thing? Team dinners?" I phrased it that way just in case he'd been thinking of something more romantic.

There was a pause on the other end of the line before he answered, "... Not really. But Agent Cartwright told me to get in touch and make sure you checked back in. I figured you might appreciate some food."

I couldn't decide if that meant Molly didn't trust me to check in or not. At the end of the day, it didn't matter much. I needed food and she was my superior. She called the shots and I was the lowest person on the totem pole. So, if she wanted me back at headquarters hanging with the only mundane agent not in the know on the case, I'd do it.

"I'm already on my way back." After a beat, I added, "I'll have whatever you're having."

As I ended the call, a sudden chill raced

up my spine, as if someone was watching me. I turned ever-so-slightly to glance over my left shoulder. I thought I caught my mother disappear into a crowd across the street. Whatever she was mixed up in was going to come back and bite me in the ass. I was just sure of it.

SEVEN

Going back through security at headquarters was faster this time. I just flashed my badge and headed upstairs. I buzzed into the cubicle farm and found Duncan sitting in the conference room alone. A paper bag of what smelled like burritos sat at the far end of the table. Given the size of the bag, either he expected me to eat my weight in Mexican food or he hadn't known what to order and gotten one of everything.

"Hey," I said, making my presence known as he was staring intently at the laptop screen in front of him.

"It's like looking for a needle in a haystack," he grumbled and closed the lid of the computer, scooting his chair to the end of the table with the food.

"If it makes you feel any better I mostly struck out today, too."

"Mostly implies there was something good that came from today," he replied and pulled out a burrito marked with a 'V' which I assumed meant vegetarian.

I rummaged through the bag until I found one that looked to be a steak and chicken combo and sat down across from him. "Well, I have a name to run through the system."

"You are doing better than me. I'm still trying to figure out how they're spoofing the camera feeds. I mean, they'd need to be some sort of tech genius."

"How do you figure?" I couldn't tell him they were using magic, but I was genuinely curious to hear how he thought they were pulling it off.

"I've looked at the systems used by every bank that's been hit. They're all different setups. You'd need to know what kind of system they used before you hit them. And I mean, I don't get why they're holding up the front of the bank while they're at it. They aren't taking anything else."

All good questions. "Well, we know they have to be doing their homework before hitting the banks. Every bank they've hit has had safety deposit boxes. It would make sense that they've done the research on the types of security systems used too." I took a bite of burrito. "I've got a freelance tech consultant who is going to take another crack at the footage and see if they left anything behind we might be missing."

Duncan set his burrito down and looked at me. "You better clear that with Agent Cartwright."

"Already did," I lied.

I figured it was better to ask forgiveness later if it meant getting any closer to finding our crew. We sat there in silence, sharing our food for a solid five minutes before both of our phones rang. I managed to get to mine first, slamming my finger against the screen to answer Jacquie's incoming call.

"You're on speaker," I said, setting the phone in the center of the table.

"We've got an active robbery in progress. I'm sending you the address now."

Food lay forgotten as Duncan and I raced from the room. He beat me to the door leading to the elevators as I pulled up the pin Jacquie had just dropped in the maps app. If we were lucky, we'd make it across town before the crew escaped.

I EXPECTED chaos when we finally made it to the scene. A couple patrol cars blocked off the cross-streets and I spotted Jacquie and Molly huddled behind the far side of their SUV. I was halfway out of the car when I felt Duncan's hand on my elbow.

"You don't want to go in there without one of these," he said, passing me a tactical vest from the back seat.

I hurriedly pulled it on over my head, keeping my back turned so he couldn't see the embarrassment on my face as we rushed to join Molly and Jacquie. I did my best to peer over the hood of the vehicle and take in the lay of the land. I didn't see anyone who looked like an obvious lookout, but if they were using Whisperers, they wouldn't be obvious.

"Are we sure it's the same crew?" I asked in a stage whisper.

"It's one of the banks on Duncan's list," Molly answered.

"We aren't just going to let them get away, are we?" I called, already reaching for the gun holstered on my hip.

"They've got hostages. We're not just rushing in there," Jacquie answered.

In that moment, I resented Duncan's presence in our group huddle. It would have been so much simpler to just offer to slip into the bank as the crew had done—unnoticed—and see what I could find out from there.

"If they stick to the pattern, no one is

going to get hurt," I protested just as the muffled sound of a gunshot came from inside followed by shouting.

So much for no injuries.

I couldn't just sit here while these assholes hurt innocent people. I closed my eyes and turned my focus inward. I found the core of my magic, burning white hot in my chest. It longed to be used. For all the trouble I'd had reining it in, it was still a thing of beauty to behold. It connected me to the world around me in a way people could only dream of. When I opened my eyes, everything around me had a gauzy haze to it. The smell of lavender blooming filled my nose. The haziness around the people closest to me all looked the same. A pale almost white halo around them. I crept around the back of the SUV and scanned the edge of the building.

Show me what's hidden.

Slowly the hazy outline of a figure standing on the far side of the building resolved into focus. I couldn't tell anything more specific about the figure other than they appeared average height. I'd never tried to use my magic to unravel someone else's invisibility, especially not from a distance. I tapped Molly on the shoulder and leaned in close. "I think I have an angle on the lookout."

"I don't see anything," she answered before clapping a hand over her mouth and mumbling, "Of course, I wouldn't."

"Let me try and get to them. If I can sneak up on them, maybe we can find out where they've been recruiting and what exactly they're after."

In my peripheral vision, the hazy outline started to shift. They were going to run. They might not know the specifics of what was happening on the inside, but they'd heard the gunshot and the screams. They knew it wasn't' good and they would be culpable for whatever happened inside.

"Please," I begged.

"Be careful and make sure no one sees you," Molly answered.

I waited until she'd moved up to whisper something in Duncan's ear before letting my magic take hold. I let it wash over me as I slid around the back of the SUV. Thankfully, everyone else's attention was focused on the front of the building. I still turned my gaze upward, clocking security cameras pointed up the street and at the front of the bank. The bulk of the SUV would give me cover and if I was careful, I wouldn't have to reveal myself until I was out of the range of the cameras.

The air around me bent to my will, almost buoying me off the ground as I sprinted across the street. The hazy figure that had been watching our collection of vehicles took a few steps away from me.

Can they sense me?

There wasn't time to ponder that. I'd never had to worry about whether other people could sense my magic, because they'd been in on the secret. I held out a hand and felt the edge of their spell. It clung tight to their form, almost like it was a second skin. Whoever this person was, they used their invisibility to a far greater extent than I ever did. It was ingrained in them, which meant they weren't going to become visible without a fight. Good thing I was up for one.

I dug my hands into the edges of the spell, forcing it to become tangible, all while keeping myself unseen to the world around me. The figure bucked against the direct assault, but I held fast.

"You're not getting away that easy," I whispered.

Moment by moment, the spell loosened around my target, and I saw a flash of dark skin—a hand and forearm. I poured out more will and my magic leapt to respond. I hadn't let it out to play in so long. It sung in my blood and bounced off nerve endings that stoked my adrenaline. *I was going to catch the bad guy, damn it.*

I poured all of my focus into unraveling the spell in front of me. Sounds and smells from the city around me vanished and all I could see was the hazy outline of the figure coming into focus. Sharp jolts of pain lanced up my fingers when I finally made contact with their hand. They were fighting back now. I pushed, forcing my will to overtake theirs. I just needed a little more and I would be able to make an ID. Their spell faltered just enough to show me the curves of a female body.

"You know I can see you," I tried, thinking approaching them as a person might help them calm down. "I just want to talk to you. I don't want to hurt you."

Their response came in the form of a fist flung at my face. I barely dodged the full force of the blow. The side of my head ached dully and I slammed a hand forward at what I estimated was head height on reflex. I felt my knuckles collide with the meaty flesh of someone's cheek, but the jolt up my arm from the contact was enough to throw me off kilter. They pulled their magic around them and disappeared. I couldn't even see the haze of their aura with my magically enhanced vision anymore.

Sights and sounds came rushing back and I doubled over as the pain hit me all at once. Heat cascaded over me from head to toe, bringing with it the acidic taste of failure and doubt. I might have graduated top of my class at the academy, but Molly had been wrong to put her trust in me. I wasn't good enough. I couldn't even stop one person from fleeing the scene of a crime. How was I supposed to help solve this crime if I couldn't even keep hold of a single person for more than a few minutes?

"Kayla? Are you there?" Molly's voice was tentative, coming from behind me.

I turned to look at her and remembered that she couldn't see me when I was actively using my magic. It took more effort than I liked to take down the barrier my magic had built up around me. Cold beads of sweat prickled along the nape of my neck as my body finally became solid again.

"I lost them," I huffed. "I'm sorry. I was trying to counteract their magic and then ... they just slipped away. I should have tried harder."

She pointed at my head. "Looks like they got a hit in."

I flexed my right hand. "I got one in, too. I don't know. Maybe we'll get lucky and they'll show up at a clinic looking for medical attention."

"You did good. Don't apologize. I may not have magic, but I've seen the toll it can take on a person. I was there that night in the hospital, remember?"

How could I forget? It had been the first time I ever tried to use my magic to conceal someone other than myself. She reached out a hand and patted my shoulder. "Promise me you aren't going to beat yourself up about this. This job isn't easy, even with the added boost you've got."

I shook out the pain in my hand and rubbed at the side of my head. "Did we get the assailants inside?"

"We've got one in custody, but when we breached the vault with the safety deposit boxes, no one was there."

I'd been so distracted by trying to catch the lookout, their safe cracker could have walked right by me, and I wouldn't have noticed. "Did they get into the box?"

Molly nodded. "It was opened, but nothing

looked to be taken. But we won't know for sure until we get a full manifest of what was inside."

"Damn it."

"Thankfully, no one was hurt inside," she said and started to lead me back to the vehicles blocking the streets. I saw Duncan loading a wiry guy into the back seat of our SUV.

"But the shot …" I trailed off.

"Security guard trying to intimidate the offender. Fired into the ceiling."

"But we've got one of them," I said, as if to remind myself that this hadn't been a complete bust. I might not have nailed the lookout, but having the front man was better. He knew what they were after. Now I just had to convince him to talk.

"You want first crack at this guy, Rookie?" Jacquie called from the other side of the second SUV.

"Don't you think someone more experienced should take the first run at him?" I gestured toward Duncan. "I mean, it would look kind of suspicious to have the newbie questioning the suspect right out of the gate."

"He knows you were brought in because you had a unique perspective and background for this case. He'd understand given the clock we're up against and how much we don't know, you asking the pertinent questions from the start is more important than appearances for the brass," Jacquie replied.

"Besides, something tells me he'd think it was kind of badass for you to lead the interrogation," Molly added with a wink.

I smiled in spite of myself. Knowing Duncan would think I was badass didn't hurt and even made his awkward attempts at flirting somewhat endearing. The moment of amusement dwindled as I realized there were other conversations I needed to have with my superiors. I knew I needed to share what I'd learned from my mother with Jacquie and Molly, but I couldn't bring myself to do it. Not yet. Not unless I couldn't get the man we now had in custody to talk. I looked to Jacquie. "Will you come in with me?"

She arched a dark brow at me. "You don't need a babysitter."

"Maybe not, but it's kind of hard to play good cop, bad cop with only one person in the room."

"If you want me in, I'll be there. Might even be like old times."

The fact that she would compare me to her old partner spoke volumes. I knew they'd had rough patches. Still I'd admired the way they'd worked together, magical and mundane. As much as Ezri had inspired me to take this step, Jacquie had been an important part, too.

Time to put my interrogation skills to the test.

JUNE 5, 2019

EIGHT

My neck was stiff by the time the clock hit midnight. Our bank robber, Corbin Wayne, had remained tight-lipped except to ask for a lawyer the minute we brought him into the interrogation room.

"Maybe it's a stall tactic," I said through a yawn as I stared at him through the viewing window outside interrogation.

"Could be, but he's entitled to have an attorney present during questioning," Jacquie answered. "We may be the feds, but we still have to abide by his rights, even if it means he's running out the clock."

"They don't tell you about this part of the job. The standing around feeling useless bit."

"It's not all about the glamour of the big bust or arrest. The real work is putting your nose to the grindstone and following the evidence, wherever it leads."

"I guess I should have known that. I mean, that was always the parts you guys needed help with. Not the flashy stuff, but the legwork."

"No one ever said this job was easy. She certainly never did," Jacquie murmured, her voice dipping on the word *'she.'*

"I didn't mean to imply that," I blurted.

"Look, I think it's admirable that she inspired you to step up and make a difference, but you're not her. No one is expecting you to be. Hell, some days, I think she'd wished she wasn't supposed to save the damn world."

"I just want to make them both proud."

"Earning that badge was a good start."

"How did you get around the whole trying to talk about magic in front of clueless lawyers with Ezri?"

Jacquie's lips quirked into a smile. "Somehow we got lucky so to speak and most of the people we interrogated about magic-related crimes also happened to be related to the Order and back then, they had lawyers on the payroll."

The Order of Samael had gone defunct as far as anyone knew years ago when their leadership was decimated by their own stupid quest for power. Whatever legal team they'd had on retainer to bail out their higher-ranking members was probably long gone, too. Which meant whoever showed up to defend Mr. Wayne would be ignorant of the existence of magic. I'd have to get creative.

If they ever fucking showed up.

"Still, I'm pretty sure those interrogations were recorded. You couldn't risk someone watching or walking by and picking up on things they weren't supposed to."

"Focus on the stuff we can prove by mundane means. He knows we apprehended him in the midst of a bank robbery. No one is going to dispute that. Start there and let him lead you. You can dig into his associates without mentioning people who can walk through walls."

A light knock on the door leading to the hallway drew my attention and Duncan stuck his head in. "Mr. Wayne's lawyer is getting buzzed up right now."

"Thanks," I replied, trying to rub the fatigue from my eyes.

"You know what you're doing. Trust your gut," Jacquie coached and handed me a water bottle.

I glanced from the bottle to Jacquie and back again in confusion. Jacquie gestured to the man sitting handcuffed to the table in the interrogation room. "A little empathy goes a long way, Good Cop."

I accepted the water and steeled myself for the conversation ahead. I hadn't graduated the top of my class at Quantico by accident. I'd proved to everyone there I could do this. I strode into the interrogation room and set the bottle of water on the table in front of Corbin.

"Here, let me undo those," I offered, pulling the handcuff key from my pocket.

"I said I wasn't talking without a lawyer," he countered brusquely as I unshackled him. He rubbed at his wrists and eyed the water warily.

"I'm just trying to make you a little more comfortable, Corbin. I know you've been in here a while. Your lawyer is on their way up right now. And I promise, it's just a bottle of water."

I took a few steps back and placed myself along the wall adjoining the door to the outside. My body posture should make it clear that I wasn't here to talk. He finally reached for the water, twisting off the cap, and taking several long gulps. I spotted the flash of something dark on the underside of his right wrist as he set the bottle down.

"You don't look like much of a Fed," he commented.

I let out a little laugh. "Yeah? And what do you think I look like?"

He shrugged. "Normal?"

That got a heartier laugh out of me. "Oh, believe me, I have never been normal. But I'll take that as a compliment."

The door opened and Jacquie walked in followed by a squat woman with sandy hair and a sour expression. The folder under her arm bore multiple names scribbled on it in barely legible handwriting. This guy had definitely not scored some high-priced lawyer on retainer. If I had to guess, more like a poor over-worked public defender.

"I trust you weren't questioning my client without counsel present." She addressed me as she sat down.

"Wouldn't dream of it," I replied and sat down across the table. Jacquie joined me.

"And what evidence do you have to hold my client?" She eyed Jacquie, as if I were no longer interesting.

"Mr. Wayne let's cut to the chase here. We arrested you during the commission of a robbery. There is no getting around that fact. We've got eyewitnesses and security footage as well as the weapon we recovered from you at the scene," she said.

Wayne's lawyer's face blanched and she leaned in, whispering something in his ear I didn't quite catch.

"You offering a deal or something?" He leaned forward; hands clasped around the water bottle.

"That depends on what you're willing to offer us in return," Jacquie replied, glancing my direction and offering up a small nod.

I leaned forward and made eye contact with him. "We know that you're working with a crew that has some very specialized skills. I get that there's honor among thieves, but you're facing some serious jail time. Unless you can give us something, your co-conspirators or the overall operations."

"Look, I'd never met them before today. That's not how it works," he said, the plastic bottle crinkling in his grasp.

"Tell me how it works then," I replied.

"I just got a call telling me where to go and when. They said not to worry about the vault.

Just keep the people up front focused on me. That's all."

"Did you get this information from a phone call or a text?" I prodded, hoping there was a call history Avery could trace.

"No, we did it during our weekly bridge meeting," he replied, his tone biting. "It was a burner cell."

"You say you've never saw the people handling the vault entry, but you had to have met them before today. We know this is linked to a series of other robberies across the city," I said.

"You aren't listening. I don't know anything about any other robberies. I was just told to show up there and keep people distracted."

That didn't fit with the pattern we'd seen so far, did it? A wave of nausea washed over me as my brain tried to focus on the conversation unfolding in the interrogation room while going back over the video evidence we had from the other banks to see if Corbin had been involved.

"Let's talk about how you got recruited.

What makes you so qualified for the role of bank robber?" Jacquie interjected.

Wayne shrugged, uncurling his fingers from around the bottle. That flash of something dark on his wrist caught my attention again. It was all I could do not to reach over and push up his sleeve to see what lay beneath the fabric. "I know some people who run in certain circles and they needed someone to do a job for them. I offered."

"Would these people be part of a certain organization that likes a little chaos out in the world?" I broached, eyeing his defense lawyer to see if she perked up at my question.

The poor woman just looked overwhelmed. She caught me looking and straightened. "I'd like a few minutes with my client to determine what information he may be able to provide you for a plea."

Jacquie held up her hands. "We'll be right outside."

I followed her out of the interrogation room, irritation hitting me now that we were out of earshot. Maybe I'd mistaken the attorney's flustered expression as something it wasn't.

"He's got some sort of tattoo or something on his wrist," I hissed to Jacquie.

Her gaze narrowed and her lips pressed into a thin line. "What kind of tattoo?"

"I don't know, I didn't get a very good look. But she shut me down as soon as I started asking questions about how he was connected to the people who were running this operation. I thought she was just some overworked public defender, but what if she's involved in the community somehow?"

"Take a breath," Jacquie said, putting a hand on my shoulder. "We have more information than we started with, and that's a good thing."

"How does knowing he got hired for this one job helpful? Or that he didn't know what was going on in the vault?"

"Because we're getting insight into how this operation is run. Before today, we assumed it was one crew hitting banks. It's bigger than we thought and the people behind it are smarter than we realized. They're giving themselves and their people plausible deniability by not using the same people each time."

"I just wish I could get him to tell us what they're after. Why those safety deposit boxes? And why even bother staging the robberies in the front of the bank of they can just walk in unseen?"

"Because in every robbery before today, they made off with some cash from the front," Molly interjected from the doorway to the exterior hallway. "My guess is that is how these guys are getting paid."

"It still seems like a huge risk to take. I mean, he's putting himself out there to be caught. Why would he agree to do that, knowing he would likely be caught in the act and face serious jail time?"

"Maybe he didn't think that far ahead? He could have been after a quick pay day," Jacquie suggested.

"Something still isn't adding up," I muttered.

"If I were putting together something on this scale, I'd definitely do it this way. You keep everyone in the dark, so they can't reveal more than the piece of the puzzle they have," Molly said.

"Maybe he doesn't have any loyalty to the other people he was with today. But he has to know something if he thinks he can bargain with us," I said, my temples beginning to throb.

A sharp knock on the door to the interrogation room cut the conversation short. The defense attorney stuck her head out long enough to say, "Unless you're offering immunity, my client isn't interested in a plea."

That's an abrupt about face.

"He should really reconsider," I blurted.

"Those are our terms," the attorney said and left the door ajar, returning to her seat beside Wayne.

Shit.

The scent of lavender tickled my nose and I balled my hands into fists. I could feel myself becoming insubstantial, the world taking on a haze that came with invisibility. If I could just get a minute or two alone with Wayne, I could show him that I had magic and maybe even convince him to help me. Short of that, I knew there were ways of getting information from people without them having to talk.

"If your client isn't willing to play ball, then we'll just send him for processing," Jacquie said abruptly, stepping back into the interrogation room and resecuring the handcuffs around Wayne's wrists.

I tried to give him a pleading look as she led him out of the room, but he averted his gaze. I studied his attorney as she gathered his folder and straightened her suit jacket. She looked less frazzled now and I half wondered if the folder with names scribbled on it was a deliberate misdirection. She wanted me to think she didn't know what was going on, so I'd share more information than I might otherwise. She was good.

"Let me know if you change your mind," she said, handing me a crisp white business card with a law firm's name I didn't recognize. So much for my public defender assumption.

My shoulders sagged as she disappeared, leaving me to stand there beside Molly. She looked as exhausted as I did and yet she still wore a look of determination. This felt like a stumbling block to me. We had one man in custody, but there were probably dozens more out there ready and willing to be the next Corbin Wayne.

"You're probably thinking you failed right about now," Molly said.

"Don't you? I crashed and burned in there."

"You didn't."

"You weren't there," I argued.

"Trust me, you didn't crash and burn. You got him to open up and you spotted his tattoo." She paused and glanced around to make sure we were alone. "Do you think it's ... that Order mark?"

"I don't know, it could be. But I mean they've been disbanded for years. Why resurface now? And I thought all the top guys got wiped out?"

"Just because the head got cut off doesn't mean the rest of the body isn't writhing around out there," she noted. "Every criminal enterprise has foot soldiers. Maybe we're dealing with someone trying to make a name for themselves."

If that was the case, they weren't doing a very good job of it. We had no clue who was really behind the robberies or what they were after. Hard to make a name for yourself if people don't even know what they're supposed to remember you for.

"Look, we're not going to get anything more done here tonight. Go home and get some rest. We'll come back at it fresh in a few hours."

I wanted to argue with her, but the yawn that escaped my lips betrayed me. I hadn't been able to pull all-nighters since college and maybe some sleep would do me good. I knew there were missing pieces to this case that I just wasn't seeing. Maybe some sleep would help me sort them out.

NINE

Sleep was not, in fact, the answer to my problems. Every time I closed my eyes, hazy figures with brands all over their bodies haunted me, chasing me down, and smothering me. So, by six o'clock, I sat at the kitchen table in my apartment downing my third cup of coffee in the last hour. At least I'd managed a quick shower and change of clothes, too. That alone had helped beat back some of the exhaustion.

Molly and Jacquie might both be feeling optimistic about catching Corbin, but I just couldn't wrap my head around how it got us any closer to our targets. It didn't offer up any other clues to predict which bank they'd hit next or when. A pang of anger hit me as my mind drifted to the thought, *what would Desmond suggest?* I was certain there was no chance I could communicate with a dead man, especially if his ever-resourceful wife hadn't managed it in the years since his death.

"You'd probably tell me to rely on the other people around me, because I don't have to have all the answers," I said to the empty air around me.

As if on cue, my phone rang on the table beside me. I glanced at it, not recognizing the number. "Special Agent Rogers," I answered.

"Damn, only a few days out of the academy and you're all business, even at the ass crack of dawn," Perri said on the other end of the line.

The tension I hadn't even realized was building in my neck muscles melted away. "Sorry, it's been a long couple of days and I haven't exactly slept much."

"That case really as big as they thought?"

"Actually, it might be. It's a lot more complex than we originally thought. It's looking like it might be a bunch of smaller connected cells operating on the say so of a larger organization. At least, that's what the guy we caught yesterday fed us." Until his lawyer had shut down our questioning.

"Sounds way more exciting than my assignment. Boring white collar fraud," she sighed.

"I'm glad you called," I said. "I missed my sparring partner."

"How's it been being back home? I know it wasn't your ideal destination."

I exhaled and set the phone down, putting it on speaker. "Parts of have been surprisingly good. The agents that requested me for this task force are people I knew before joining the bureau. So, it's been cool getting to work with them in a different way."

"And some parts have been horrible?" she prodded.

"Well, I wasn't expecting my boyfriend to get out of jail and break up with me," I said, my breath hitching in my throat at the end of the sentence.

"Oh, shit, Kayla. I'm so sorry to hear that. I mean the break-up, obviously not the getting out of prison thing. That's good, right?"

"Yeah, it is. I mean, I never thought he should have been locked up in the first place, but it wasn't my call. But yeah, the break-up hurt. And then I ran into my mom who admitted …" I stopped short. I couldn't tell her that my mother's magic had turned on her just like mine had on me. Perri didn't know about magic and there was no way I was spilling that particular secret over the phone at six in the morning on zero sleep. "She admitted she'd been diagnosed with mental health issues. I think she was hoping it would excuse her being a shitty parent when I was growing up."

"Again, I'm sorry. Sounds like being home is kind of dredging up the past for you in a lot of ways."

"More than I thought it would." Between Kevin and my mother, it had been an emotionally wrought couple of days. Not to mention feeling like I wasn't living up to Ezri and Desmond's expectations of who and what I could be.

"Well, when this case is over, maybe we can meet up for a girls' weekend."

Her suggestion brought a smile to my face. "That would be nice. But something tells me this job is going to keep both of us busy for a long while."

"Having plans, even tentative ones, sometimes helps combat the drudgery of life," she noted.

"Yeah, I guess it does."

My sleep-deprived brain began spinning, trying to envision a time when we could actually reconnect. I imagined us sitting in some hole-in-the-wall bar chatting over a beer. The vision in my head shifted, replaced with the interior of Notre Dame and I let out a gasp.

"You okay, Kayla?" Perri's voice sounded distant.

"Yeah, I just realized something about my case. I need to go. I'll talk to you later and I promise, we'll find time to put that girls' weekend on the books."

I hung up and nearly fumbled my phone off the table in my haste to pick it up. I sent a text to Molly, letting her know I was heading to the office after making one other stop. Jonathan may have insisted he didn't know anything about the robberies, but that didn't mean our culprits didn't still use his bar as a base of operations and a recruitment ground. I had no idea how I was going to sweet talk him into giving me video footage, but I had to try.

I SHOULD HAVE ENLISTED BACKUP. **He'd** practically steamrolled me on our last visit. Despite that I was in such a rush to follow this potential lead; I'd just gotten on the train and thrown all reason to the wind. Except I was a fully qualified FBI Agent, damn it. He had to respect that.

The lines of college kids I'd come to expect outside the establishment were gone by the time I arrived a little before seven. The bouncer wasn't out front, but the front door was unlocked. I walked in, making sure my badge was visible. The scent of spilled alcohol and stale food hit my nose as I stepped into the bar proper. The space was empty save for a figure down at the end of the bar. I should see a shoulder. Even when he used a glamour to conceal himself, the bartender was a hulking figure.

"Jonathan?" I called.

The figure stood and turned to reveal a young woman, around my age. She wore a sleeveless top with her hair piled on the top of her head in a messy bun. "Sorry, he's not here right now. And we're not really open."

I held up my badge. "Maybe you could help me …?" I trailed off, hoping the air of authority I gave off would prompt her to give me her name.

"Misty."

"So, Misty, the bar has security cameras, right?"

Her glance off to her right at the tiny lens mounted above the doorway was all the answer I needed. "Look, this place doesn't have problems that the FBI needs to worry about."

"I'm not saying that the owner has done anything wrong. I just have reason to believe some people we are looking for may have used this place as a cover to meet. I was hoping I could take a look at the security footage just for the last couple of weeks."

She set down the rag in her hand. "I'm just helping out my uncle for a couple of weeks. I don't really have authority to do anything."

I leaned on the bar. "I think we both know your uncle's stance on law enforcement. He'd rather we stay out of his place of business."

Nervous laughter bubbled in her throat. "Sounds about right." After a beat she added, "You kind of remind me of this other cop I helped once."

"I'm sure whoever that was appreciated your help," I said.

"Look, he's out doing a supply run, so he won't be back for like an hour. I don't know how much footage he actually has, but I can try."

"Thank you, Misty."

I moved to the far end of the bar while she came around and led me into the small back office with a single computer. I scanned the walls, looking for an obvious hiding place for the safe, but nothing stood out. Leave it to Jonathan to probably keep his hard-earned money under a mattress or something.

"So, how far back did you want?'

"The last two or three weeks if you can."

"What did these guys do?"

"Bank robberies." It was all she would get out of me and it seemed to be enough to get her to focus on the task at hand.

I waited as she clicked through video files and copied them onto a flash drive. Her hand shook slightly as she handed it over. "Please promise this isn't going to get Uncle Jonathan in trouble."

"As long as your uncle wasn't involved, he's got nothing to worry about," I replied and pocketed the drive.

Time to head to the office and start combing through footage. Plus, I had bank security feeds to review to see if Corbin's insistence that yesterday's attempted heist was his only involvement.

I expected Molly to be in given my earlier text and yet the office was eerily quiet when I entered. Though I could see lights on in the conference room. Someone was here. I nudged open the door to find Duncan leaning over a laptop on the table. When he looked up, I could see the bags under his eyes from across the room.

"You couldn't sleep either?" I noted and stepped into the room.

"No," he answered, stifling a yawn. "I've been trying to go over the footage we had from the robberies, following up to see if our suspect was telling the truth."

"Great minds," I said and settled beside him. "Any luck yet?"

"Well, we don't have clear footage from the first bank," he said, turning the laptop so I could see the screen. It was fuzzy at best.

Maybe they'd tried to take out the cameras and hadn't managed. "But the person right there is our robber."

I squinted at the fuzzy figure he indicated. I could see the shape of the gun in their hand, but I noticed they were left handed and I was fairly certain Corbin was right-handed. He'd picked up the water bottle with his right hand. "I agree, the footage is crap, but it doesn't look like our guy."

"The footage from the second bank is clearer. This one looks like it could be a closer match to Wayne, but he never turns to look at the camera," Duncan said, flipping images.

"What about the third?" I prompted.

"I was just getting to it when you came in," he said and tapped on another window and hit 'Play.'

We watched as the figure entered the bank and approached the counter. They passed the teller a note and I could see the butt of the gun protruding from the back of their pants. Except this person was clearly female.

"Okay, so we've got at least two other

people. But we can't say for sure that the people trying to break into the vaults weren't the same," I said.

"We still don't have an explanation for how that's even happening. Like we said before, different banks, different systems. Did your contact have any luck digging into things?"

I hadn't touched base with Avery in a while. "I'll check in," I answered and held up the flash drive from Misty. "I paid a visit to an old acquaintance and managed to get security footage from Notre Dame the last few weeks."

"How's that help?"

"Well, he may not be involved in any of this, but a crowded bar seems like a decent place to try doing business. I was hoping we'd find Corbin on camera there and find out who he was meeting with."

"Worth a shot."

He inserted the drive into the laptop, bringing up yet another video window. As he sat down, I heard his stomach rumble and mine followed suit. "Hey, you've been at this all night. Why don't you go grab some coffee and breakfast? I'll see what I can find here," I suggested.

"Okay. But only if you let me buy you breakfast, too," he answered with a shy smile.

"That would be nice. Thanks."

"Want anything in particular?"

"Surprise me."

He flashed another smile before he got up and grabbed his suit jacket off the back of the chair. I knew he didn't need it outside—it was already in the sixties—but I suspected he was using it to hide the wrinkles in his shirt. It was kind of cute. Turning my attention to the files he'd loaded, I settled in my chair and hit 'Play.'

Nothing looked suspicious at first. Just lots of barely dressed college kids grinding on the dance floor. Except three days ago, Corbin strode in and took a seat at the bar. Without the benefit of audio, I couldn't hear what he and Jonathan talked about. Though by the way the hulking bartender set down the bottle of beer and moved down the way, I assumed he was just trying to keep his customers plied with alcohol.

I tracked Corbin as he sat at the bar and watched the people dancing. I thought he might have been eyeing a slender-framed male figure at one of the high top tables. Only it was just out of frame and I couldn't make out facial features. I waited to see what Corbin did. After five minutes, he left the bottle of beer unattended on the bar and wove his way through the crowd to that out-of-frame figure.

"Why doesn't this stupid thing have audio?" I griped. Logistically I knew it wouldn't be of any use. All I'd end up with was the bass from the music and white noise from the vocals and myriad voices. But as he stepped back into frame, I saw something slide into his pocket. A burner phone perhaps?

"I got you a muffin and scone, because I wasn't sure which you'd prefer," Duncan announced returning with a white paper bag and travel tray with two cups of coffee on it.

"Thanks," I said as I accepted the bag and

one of the cups. "It looks like Corbin was telling the truth, that he was recruited at least. I just saw him take what looks like a burner phone from some guy at the bar."

I tracked Corbin's movements as he stopped at the bar and slid money under the bottle before disappearing completely. *Why did I have to be right*? Knowing that these lunatics were recruiting at the bar meant I'd be spending even more time at old haunts; places I never wanted to be again.

Before Duncan could say anything, my phone rang, disrupting the quiet of the conference room. I glanced at the display and said, "It's Agent Cartwright." I answered the call. "Morning."

"We're moving Wayne to lock-up. I thought you might like to come along for the ride. Might give you a chance to impress upon him the severity of his actions."

I wasn't entirely sure what she was alluding to, but I'd take another shot at Corbin without his lawyer present. I knew nothing he told me would be admissible in court, but the questions I intended to ask weren't things that belonged out in the general public anyway.

TEN

I offered Duncan a quick apology as I rushed out of the conference room. I downed the scone in the elevator as I awkwardly balanced the to-go cup in my other hand. I was sure I got side-eye from the guard behind the front desk as I brushed crumbs from my jacket and headed outside. I spotted Molly leaning on the passenger side door of a tinted SUV.

"You look more awake than I would have thought," she quipped.

"Caffeine will do that for a person," I answered and tried to peer through the windows without luck. I let out a tiny bit of will, lavender wafting from my pores as the glass shimmered and for the briefest moment it vanished to reveal an empty back seat.

"I thought we were transporting him," I said.

"Relax, Rookie, he's over there," Jacquie replied, stepping around the back of the SUV and gesturing to another SUV.

"We're going to have maybe twenty minutes during transport, so you're going to need to make it count," Molly explained.

"What exactly are you expecting me to do?"

"Let him in on your little secret, maybe it will get him to open up," Molly suggested.

"Or you could always take a stroll through his head," Jacquie said.

I failed to repress a shiver. I'd only ever seen that done as an outside observer. I'd never actually gone through another person's memories. I wasn't sure I could even handle going through my own mental shit. "I'll see what I can do," I answered and started for the transport SUV.

"Duncan have any luck with that footage?" Molly called as she trailed after me.

"Not all of the footage is clear, but it looks like there were at least two other people involved. Whether it's a completely different crew or they were just rotating positions is hard to tell." I climbed into the passenger seat of the transport SUV, securing the seatbelt over my lap.

"Well, it's better than nothing," Molly said and revved the engine.

I glanced over my shoulder at Corbin. He looked bleary-eyed and more disheveled than he had when we'd parted ways six hours ago. "Holding not to your liking?"

"My lawyer said I shouldn't say anything," he said, his hands clasped tightly together in front of him.

"Sounds like you just ignored the advice of counsel," I snickered as the SUV ahead of us pulled away from the building and our vehicle followed suit. I caught a third SUV fall into formation behind us.

Corbin sunk back as far as his shackles would allow and gazed out the window. The metal mesh separating him from the front of the SUV cast ripples of morning sun across his face.

"You know, part of your story checks out. You should be happy about that," I said in a conversational tone. "I mean, you're still going to prison for a very long time. It doesn't seem fair that this all falls on you."

"I guess there really is honor among thieves," Molly noted.

"I'd like to know what sort of people are worth throwing your life away for, because I haven't met anyone I'd go that far for. That's dedication. Or stupidity," I continued.

"You don't know what you're talking about," Corbin scoffed.

"I'm pretty sure I've got some idea. I don't mean to sound rude, but you don't seem the planner type. Foot soldier, sure, but you're no mastermind. Whoever is pulling your puppet strings has more power than you want to admit. I'm guessing it's the kind most people wouldn't even believe exists."

"You're crazy, lady," he said.

I needed to get a good look at the mark I'd noticed on his wrist this morning. If I could confirm he was part of the Order, that would give me some clue about who we were dealing with.

"I've been called a lot of things in my life, crazy doesn't come close to the worst," I retorted and turned enough in my seat to face him without the seatbelt digging into my shoulder. *Time for a little show and tell.*

My magic leapt to the forefront of my mind the instant I decided it was time to use it. It had been waiting there since I'd peered through the window, longing to take charge. It slipped down my left arm and wrapped around my hand like a glove fit just to me. I reached backward and my hand faded, passing through the partition. My fingers hooked into the length of chain between the shackles around his wrists and yanked him forward as far as he could go. The motion was enough to dislodge the fabric around his right wrist. The mark I'd noticed was just a mole.

"Where is it?" I demanded.

"The fuck!" he yelped, trying desperately to pull away from me. "Your hand went ... invisible."

Shit, did I just reveal magic to a mundane criminal?

"And I can do far worse than that," I bluffed, praying the scare might loosen his lips.

"Look, I swear, I didn't know the guy who hired me. He just told me where to show up and when. He said all I had to do was go in and keep the tellers and guards distracted. I'd get to keep whatever money they gave me so long as I didn't get caught."

"So, you never saw the people breaking into the vault?"

"No. They wanted it kept that way, like I told you. Look, I'm an asshole, but that's all I know."

"Where'd you meet this guy who hired you?" I already knew the answer.

"Some bar out near the colleges. One time. He gave me the phone and texted me the instructions."

"I'm going to ask you a very important question and I need you to answer it honestly," I said, fighting to keep my composure.

"Okay. Sure."

"What I just did was magic. Literal magic. You've never seen or done anything like that before?"

"No way. You think if I could do shit like that, I'd be walking into a bank with my face plastered all over the cameras?"

He had a point. "Your boss tell you to go in unmasked?"

"Look, I shouldn't be telling you any of this," he murmured.

I pulled my hand back through the partition, watching as my fingers and palm became solid again. "If you only met this guy one time, why are you protecting him? We want him, not you."

"I'm done talking," he said and slumped back against his seat.

I looked out the windshield as the SUV eased to a stop. The occupants of the vehicle ahead of us stepped out and I realized we'd reached our destination. I jabbed at the seatbelt release and opened the door harder than necessary in my frustration. I caught Molly as she mouthed, 'Take a breath' at me before she climbed from the driver's seat and pulled Corbin out the back of the SUV.

I took slow inhales and blew them out through my mouth. Each one let the anger ebb from the surface of my emotions. Lashing out wasn't going to help the situation. I'd already exposed magic to one person today who was now a danger since he knew the truth. I wasn't about to risk letting the other agents who'd come with us in on the secret, too.

Prison officers appeared and Molly handed Corbin over to them. His face was still pale from what he'd seen me do. As they led him away, it dawned on me where we were. I knew one person locked up in this facility who had intimate knowledge of the Order's inner workings.

"Whatever you're thinking of doing, don't," Molly warned.

"How do you …" I trailed off. "It probably wouldn't be worth it anyway. Every other lead I've followed so far has dead-ended."

"You didn't expect this job to be easy, did you?" her tone was sharper than I'd ever heard her use before.

"Of course not. I just figured, because of my extra skillset, it would have gotten us closer to solving this case."

"You remind me more of her than I like to admit," Jacquie piped up. "She never said it outright, but I'm pretty sure she thought she could solve our first big case together by sheer will and magic."

"She managed it if I remember right," I noted.

"Not without some mistakes along the way. Or did you forget about the fact you had to pick her up off the floor and heal some nasty magical injuries?"

I had forgotten that. I'd built Ezri up as larger-than-life in my head after seeing what she had accomplished in such a short amount of time. I'd forgotten the struggles she'd gone through to get to that point.

"Well, I was wrong about the Order connection. At least, with Corbin specifically. The mark I thought was their brand was just a mole. And he freaked out when he saw me use magic."

"Could his memory have been altered?"

"Maybe. There's definitely something he's not telling us. He all-but confirmed he didn't know the person who hired him. There had to be a reason he was willing to go to prison for a stranger. I mean why would anyone, no matter the promise of a big score, walk into a bank with the intent of robbing it and show their face?"

"Sounds like you ought to do some more digging into his past. Maybe he's got some other connection to our ring leader he's not willing to share yet," Molly suggested.

I also ought to check in with Avery. She hadn't reached out to tell me if she'd found anything magical in the footage Duncan had been reviewing. If Corbin really had no connection to magic and he didn't have any information on how the vault was being robbed, then maybe the other people that had been hired as the face of the operation were mundane too.

"Did we ever figure out what was in the boxes at the other banks in town? Do we have any guess about what they might be after?"

Jacquie and Molly shook their heads. "Despite our insistence it would be highly beneficial for them to cooperate, the last few banks are holding out, citing customer privacy," Jacquie answered.

Damn.

"Look, I'm going to follow up with one more tech angle and see what I can unearth about Corbin."

"And what tech angle is that?" Jacquie probed.

"I sort of gave Avery over at headquarters a copy of the surveillance footage yesterday, just to see if there was anything magical going on."

Jacquie smiled. "Haven't seen her in a while ..." After a pause, she added, "Take Duncan with you."

I stopped short. "I don't think that's such a good idea. Where I'm going, there are certain conversations that need to happen and it's safer he isn't involved in them."

"He's a good agent and a good person. Top of his class, too. He's going to figure it out sooner or later," Molly replied.

I swallowed the lump of fear choking me as I climbed into the passenger seat of the transport SUV. I wasn't looking forward to the thought of having to work around Duncan's ignorance.

"Do you ever wish you hadn't found out about magic?" I broached as Molly merged into traffic and slipped into the HOV lane, heading back into the city.

"I think I always knew there was something else out there in the world, even if I hadn't seen it with my own eyes until it happened. So, no, to answer your question, I don't wish I'd never known. It has allowed me to put more bad guys behind bars and it gave me the experience of working with talented officers I never would have grown to consider friends."

I stayed quiet as she accelerated. Could I get lucky and find that Duncan, too, had some sort of natural affinity for magic users? I didn't want to send him screaming for the hills, because he did seem like a decent guy and a good agent.

"If it helps, I think she was really nervous bringing me in on her secret ... But she still did and it worked out. Not everything about your magic is going to have negative repercussions," Molly noted.

I appreciated her trying to bolster my spirits. Though I couldn't put into words just how much of a struggle it had been and continued to be to keep hold of my magic instead of letting it take the reins of my life.

"Thanks."

"Let me know what you find," she said when we reached FBI headquarters.

"What are you doing?" I paused, the vehicle door half open.

"I'm going to see if I can convince our friends at the remaining banks to part with the information they are trying to protect."

"Good luck."

I didn't expect Duncan to still be combing through video footage when I returned, but he still sat there, eyes even blearier than when I'd left him. "Hey, I have something I need to follow up on. Agent Cartwright wanted you to come with," I said. "Next round of coffee's on me."

That perked him up. He scrubbed at his face and tossed the empty coffee cup and bag in the trash. I pointed to the flash drive still protruding from his laptop.

"Bring that. We're going to need it."

"Yes, Ma'am." He answered with another shy smile, although this one verged on flirty.

As we made our way back downstairs and to his car, I braced myself. My two worlds were about to collide, and I had no idea how I was going to handle it.

ELEVEN

"So, where exactly are we going?" Duncan asked as we reached the exit that would take us to Authority headquarters.

"Uh, we have an outside technical consultant whose working on the bank surveillance footage. I'm hoping she can cross reference the footage I got from the bar and see if anyone else matches."

"I thought we had analysts for that," he said with a noncommittal shrug.

"We do, but she has some special skills and programs that our techs just don't have.

Agents DeWitt and Cartwright have worked with her on cases before."

"Got it." He glanced my direction as I pointed out the next turn. "Out of curiosity, how did you manage to get that bar footage? We didn't have a warrant."

"I might have impressed upon the owner's very nice niece that we were after some very nasty people and she offered to help."

"Impressive."

"Not really. I was just nice to her and I think she wanted to be helpful." The entrance to the circular drive came up fast on our right. I pointed and directed, "Turn here."

The tires squealed as he made a sharp turn into the driveway and pulled in behind a four-door sedan. I sent up a little prayer to the universe that we wouldn't walk into a very loud discussion on the morality of using magic.

"This place looks …." Duncan trailed off as I ushered him up the front steps and into the foyer.

"Stuffy and pretentious?" I offered.

"More like a historical society's base of operations than a tech consultant's."

He wasn't wrong. There were centuries of history in this place. Magic from thousands of practitioners clung to every surface in the building. It was part of the fabric of the Authority and its safest space.

"If she's in, she'd be upstairs," I said, giving my companion a shove between the shoulder blades and directed him to the stairs.

"Are you sure this isn't a museum or something?" he said, his tone dropping as we walked through the Council Chamber room.

"I promise, it's not. Now come on."

I pushed the door to the tech hub open and exhaled with relief. Avery sat at the computer, immersed in some task I couldn't discern. Her headphones were absent.

"Hey, Avery," I said loudly.

No reply.

I stepped forward, tapping her on the shoulder. She jumped and spun, catching her glasses before they flew off her face from the centrifugal momentum. I spotted tiny earbuds in her ears. She popped them out.

"Sorry, I didn't hear you come in. I know I haven't called, been busy upgrading security around here."

"Something I should know?"

"Uh," her gaze shifted to my mundane shadow. I gave a slight shake of my head. "It can wait."

She stood and offered a hand to Duncan, as if I hadn't spoken. "Avery Fellowes, Tech Consultant."

"Special Agent Finley Duncan," he replied, shaking her hand.

Avery smirked and turned to me. "I didn't think you'd need to bring backup just to check on me."

"They say teamwork makes the dream work, right?" I retorted.

Avery quirked a brow at me and shook her head. "Well, I'm afraid I don't have much to report. There was nothing off about the footage that I could determine. It's possible that your thieves had some sort of knowledge of the system and stuck to the blind spots to avoid being caught on camera."

"That doesn't explain how they were able to get into the safety deposit boxes without the keys," Duncan interjected.

Avery held up her hands. "I'm just the tech girl. I don't do hacking of physical things."

I held out the flash drive. "I managed to get some footage of where we believe the crew is getting their assignments. Do you think you could cross reference this with the surveillance video, see if you can pick up any of the same people?"

"Let me get this straight. You want me to basically play Where's Waldo with people I'm not even sure of what they look like? You do know I'm not a miracle worker, don't you?"

"If anyone can figure out a way to do it, it's you," I replied, trying to butter her up and also suggest she use a little magic to aid the process.

"I'll see what I can do."

I turned to Duncan. "Could you give us a minute?"

"I'm assuming this isn't case related" he replied.

"You can just wait in the room out there. I'll be right out."

He didn't look pleased at being dismissed, but he didn't argue. Thirty seconds later, Avery and I were alone in the tech hub.

"So, want to fill me in on what you couldn't say in front of him?" I prompted.

She sat down in her chair, turning the flash drive over in her hands. "I wasn't hiding anything. There wasn't anything magical that had been done to the footage."

"You're absolutely sure? You know we're dealing with Whisperers."

"I've seen their magic on security footage before. There wasn't anything that would indicate they went invisible once they were inside the bank. So, there'd be nothing to make the feed glitch," Avery answered.

"Whoever these guys are, they're smart. They're keeping the players separate. They're recruiting mundanes and Whisperers to do their dirty work." I paused and looked around the room. "Is that why you're upgrading security?"

"Look, it's probably nothing, but I just got this feeling that our technical security needed a few upgrades. I mean, we know that Whisperers don't show up on video feeds when they're invisible. I ran some tests on some old footage I had of Lola and they don't show up on infrared either. It looks like they give off more of a dispersed heat signature."

"What do you mean it disperses the heat signature?"

She swiveled in her chair and tapped a few buttons. She brought up footage I'd never seen before and hit play. I saw the back of a woman's head vanish along with a girl beside her. The bottom dropped out of my stomach as I realized what I was watching. Avery rewound the footage a few frames, so Lola reappeared. She flipped the display to show hot and cold, and I could see her heat signature still in general human form.

"Watch," Avery instructed and hit play again.

I waited and sure enough the heat signature spread out into the air around where she'd been. It faded into the heat signatures of other people in the crowd.

"So, you're installing heat sensors in the building?" I prompted.

"Among other things," she answered vaguely.

"You don't honestly think anyone is going to attack here?" I questioned, shock coloring my tone.

"You never know. It's better to be prepared."

"Take it from someone who spent a lot of her youth paranoid that something was coming. It isn't all it's cracked up to be."

She gave me an apologetic look before gesturing to the partially open door. "So, you've got yourself a mundane partner, huh?"

"He's not my partner. We're just working a case as part of a larger team," I replied.

"He's cute," she noted.

"You're married," I teased.

"Widowed and I'm allowed to window shop."

"Molly and Jacquie think I should let him in on the whole magic exists secret."

"That is kind of a big deal," Avery whispered.

"I know. I mean, I accidentally already did it with a suspect. So, my track record isn't great to begin with."

"You don't think he could handle it?"

"I don't know. That's the thing. I don't really know him. Hell, I didn't even know his first name until he told you!"

"Maybe they want you to get to know him before you break the news. He might be more inclined to believe you if he knows Kayla the normal person."

"Maybe. Why does magic have to complicate everything?" I grumbled.

"Because as amazing as magic is, it's still just a part of being human. And humans are complicated," she replied. "Speaking of, you better go find him before he starts digging through things he shouldn't."

My heart hammered against my ribs as I darted out of the room. I was so focused on what Avery might not have been able to share in front him that I hadn't realized that he could have easily wandered off and stumbled into magic I wouldn't be able to explain away. Much to my relief, I found him standing at the windows in the Council Chamber, staring down at the circular drive as people got into their cars with young children.

"So, what is this place, really?" he asked when I stepped up beside him.

"It's kind of a community center, I guess," I said. It was true. Just not for the type of community he was envisioning.

"That has a tech consultant that works with law enforcement?"

"Everyone has their hobbies," I offered as I studied the people down below. Having spotted a familiar face, a wave of anger cascaded over me. "Excuse me for a minute."

I didn't give him a chance to respond before I was halfway down the stairs. The front door opened and there he was. Kevin stood there, looking at me in surprise that quickly faded.

"What are you doing here?" My voice was sharper than I meant it to be.

"I told you, I'm trying to figure out where I fit," he replied softly.

Part of me wanted to remind him that he no longer had magic, so he shouldn't be here. But that was cruel of me. Even without magic, he was still part of this world. Just because his powers had been stripped from him didn't mean his knowledge had.

"Right, I just meant, like right now," I said.

"There's a support group for people who had the same thing happen," he pointed to a small sign on the library door I hadn't noticed on my way in.

I descended the rest of the stairs and studied the sign. Every week they held an early morning and an evening session for those whose magic had been stripped. I could hear voices inside the room and when I opened it, I found people who'd once been on the Council sitting around the long table. J.T.

Somers sat at the head of it. Our gazes met and he gave me a broad smile.

"Hey stranger. Long time no see."

He stepped out of the room and spotted Kevin. "Hey, I'm glad you were able to make it. You can head in. I'll be there in a minute to get started."

Kevin lingered by the front door, clearly uncertain if he should leave the two of us alone. Hoping to put him at ease, I pulled J.T. into an awkward one-armed hug. It was enough for Kevin to start for the open library doors.

"I thought I heard you'd gone off to join the ranks of superheroes," J.T. teased.

"I'm no superhero," I answered. "But I did finally decide to get my shit together and do something useful with my life."

"Well, authority looks good on you."

"So, how'd you know about Kevin? He only got out yesterday."

"Avery may have let it slip and she may have hacked your phone to get me his number. I figured after everything he'd been through; he could use some support."

"I'm glad he's getting help," I murmured. "I'm surprised you've got the time to run something like this, though."

"Well, I realized that I was putting my career as a medic ahead of my role as a healer here and my priorities shifted a little. I'm not Des, but I still feel like I'm helping them cope."

"That's good to hear. I really am sorry I kind of ghosted you guys after everything."

"You needed time and space to figure things out for yourself, too. No one faulted you for that."

"Thanks. You know, I was trying to avoid coming back home after graduation, but I'm starting to think the universe needed me to be here."

"Oh?"

"Just this case we're working. It feels linked to me."

"Aren't you going to introduce me to all your friends?" Duncan said as he stepped off the bottom step.

My voice caught in my throat for a moment as Kevin reappeared in the doorway. Maybe he was still jumpy about being out of the loop for so long or maybe he could sense I had some connection to Duncan. Either way, in that moment, I wished he still had magic and could have disappeared. "Right, sorry. Special Agent Duncan, this is J.T. Somers, he's a paramedic in the city and this is Kevin Ellery. My ex-boyfriend."

"You're working," Kevin said abruptly.

"Yeah." As I studied the man I thought would be in my life for years to come, a thought took form in the back of my mind. It seemed pretty clear that Corbin had a criminal history and I had to assume the others our mastermind recruited had done time, too. Whether the Whisperers were in the system was up in the air. If our ringleader had knowledge of the magical world, they could be preying on recently changed practitioners. But Kevin had still been in prison when the crimes began. Maybe he'd heard something that might help. "Do you have plans after your meeting?"

"Not really. I'm crashing at my mom's place and it's not like I've had time to find a job in the last twenty-four hours. Not that I have high expectations there. Why?"

"I'm clearly missing something here," Duncan said.

I opened my mouth to speak, but Kevin beat me to it. "Oh, she didn't tell you. I'm also a recently paroled ex-con."

I watched Duncan's face as he processed that information. His jaw worked like he wanted to form words, but nothing came out. The information was clearly not what he'd been expecting.

"It's a complicated case and he really shouldn't have been locked up in the first place," I said in a hurried breath.

"Not that it's any of my business, but I'm pretty sure our bosses frown upon dealing with personal business in the middle of an investigation," Duncan said when he'd found his voice again.

"My interest in his whereabouts for later is case related, I promise," I said, and to Kevin, I added, "I take it you've still got my number."

"Just because I need some space doesn't mean I don't ever want to see or talk to you again. So, yeah, I've still got your number."

"Good, text me when you're done, and I'll tell you where to meet us."

"Again, why?"

"Because I think you might be able to help us crack this case wide open."

Now all I had to do was explain my ex's criminal history without mentioning all the bits about wayward magic.

TWELVE

I'd never felt more ready to get out of the Authority's inner sanctum than I did right now. I was already in the passenger seat of Duncan's car by the time he slid behind the wheel.

"Sorry if I made that weird in there," he started, putting the car into drive.

"I'm the one who should be apologizing to you. I didn't mean to drag you into my baggage, especially without a heads up."

"Why do I get the feeling this is more than just a community center?"

"Uh, well, I mean they do some education

stuff and support groups, like you saw. Well, someone that used to work there kind of saved my life and helped put me on the path to becoming an agent."

"Sounds like a really nice place," he commented.

"It can be a little judgmental sometimes," I answered.

I'd known about the Authority my entire life. I'd even been to a few magic lessons there in my youth, but it had never felt like a place that wanted me as a child. It certainly hadn't been so supportive when my magic turned on me. In the Authority's eyes, Whisperers were seen as victims of their own making. Not bad people necessarily, but the people who used to be in power believed we were deserving of our fate in a way. I'd stayed connected thanks to Desmond, not because of their bureaucratic bullshit.

"So, you dated an ex-con, huh?" he continued.

"It's complicated. We met in college and then he went off the grid for a while. When he showed back up, an asshole FBI agent coerced him into doing some pretty messed up things. He paid the price for another man's ego. If I'd had any say in the matter, he wouldn't have spent a day behind bars."

"I heard rumors at the academy about an agent that went rogue, tried to kill a cop. That wouldn't happen to be the same person, would it?"

"Yep. In fact, that cop he tried to kill was one of the people who really pushed me to get my shit together and apply to Quantico in the first place."

"They must have been proud," he noted as he pulled into the flow of traffic heading into the city. We were about hit some serious rush-hour traffic.

My breath hitched. "She died in the line of duty, but I do like to think she would have approved of my career choices."

"Damn, I'm sorry."

"Don't be. She knew what she was getting into." I couldn't tell him she'd literally been fated to die. That was veering way too close into spilling the magical beans territory.

"So, how do you think your ex can help us figure out how our mastermind is recruiting folks?"

I spotted a sign for a diner at the next exit. "How about I fill you in over some real coffee and breakfast?"

"Sounds good to me."

THE DINER WAS SPARSELY POPULATED as the clock ticked closer to ten o'clock. We were inching towards brunch territory, but the server was more than happy to offer us the breakfast menu when we sat down. I pulled up the laptop Duncan had tossed in the back seat of the car and searched available records for Corbin's criminal history.

"Well, I'll give Corbin one thing. He certainly sticks to what he's good at," I said, angling the computer so we could both see it without sharing the information with the rest of the restaurant. "Seven arrests for assault and battery. One conviction that landed him in prison for a year. Paroled a month ago."

"Not a stretch to jump to armed robbery. But he had to know that getting caught with his record would get him a harsher sentence this time around. Still doesn't explain why he'd be willing to take that rap for a total stranger," he said.

"No, it doesn't," I agreed.

I turned my attention to the other records we had access to. He'd apparently started his life of crime early. There were a few juvenile court records that had been sealed. Though others were still accessible, including records about his family. He'd been taken from a father who struggled with substance abuse. His mother did not appear to be in the picture, and he had an older sister.

Foster care records showed that the pair had been placed in a couple of group homes together before his sister aged out of the system.

"Looks like he's got a sister he might be

close with," I noted, flipping back to his sheet. I spotted her name as a witness on a couple of the charges, including the one that had landed him in prison. "Seems like they're still in each other's lives. He went to jail for beating up an abusive boyfriend."

"If whoever roped him in is threatening the safety of his family, that could be a strong motivator for taking the charge and keeping quiet."

"Should we bring her in, see what she knows?" I suggested.

"I mean, we don't have many other leads to go on at this point. Unless your analyst friend can identify anyone else from the surveillance footage. Or if Agents Cartwright or DeWitt have luck loosening the banks' security, we're dead in the water."

Figuring out how they recruited the front man was one thing, but I still couldn't picture what they had over the Whisperers to get them to use their magic in service for someone else. Then again, it hadn't taken much peer pressure to get me to do things I knew were wrong in the past.

"You know they brought me in on this case, because I have some unique experience related to what's happening, right?"

"That's about all I know. And that you were top of your class, so you're smart and resourceful."

"Thanks. Well, I didn't exactly have the saintliest past. I had brushes with the criminal justice system. Nothing that ever stuck, and I never would have done anything that would have physically hurt people. But I went through something kind of traumatic in college, not long after Kevin fell off the face of the earth actually." Or more accurately got turned into a stone gargoyle trapped down at the Public Garden. "I fell in with the wrong people, but they had the kind of skills to attempt something like our thieves."

"Do you think it could be anyone from your past?"

"I doubt it. The ones that aren't dead, are either in jail or they skipped town and know that if they ever showed their face here again, they'd be locked up."

The server came by and refilled our coffee cups then set down a plate of eggs and sausage in front of Duncan, and an omelet in front of me. I dug into the food, not to satiate a hunger, but to avoid the question I sensed was coming. For his part, Duncan made a show of eating some of his food before he spoke again.

"So, you must have a theory on how they're getting into the vaults undetected. Especially if it's a new crew each time."

Magic.

There was no other explanation I could offer that he would just believe me without him calling me on my bullshit. I'd already freaked out one person today by sharing the truth about who and what I was. However, I shouldn't be ashamed of the fact that I am a witch. It's in my blood, as immutable as my DNA.

"I do have a theory, but if I tell you, you're going to think I'm crazy."

"Have you shared the theory with Agents DeWitt or Cartwright?"

I nodded mutely.

"Do they think you're crazy?"

"Well, no."

"Then why would I think you were crazy?'

"Because they have other information that you don't. Information about me and things in my past."

He set down his utensils. "How about you tell me, and we see where it goes? If it helps us catch a crew of thieves, I'm open to pretty much anything."

This is really happening. Just go for it.

"They're using magic to walk through the walls and not be seen."

I watched his expression. He wasn't screaming or running away, and he wasn't laughing hysterically at me either. He sat there calmly, turning the fork handle over between his fingers.

"So, you're telling me people just what, snap their fingers and can turn into a ghost then pass through walls?"

"No. There's generally no snapping involved, and they aren't dead. And not everyone can do it. Well, I guess theoretically anyone with magic *could* do it, but there's certain people whose magic acts as sort of a constant invisibility spell."

"So, you're asking me to believe in supernatural criminals, because regular ones aren't scary enough?"

"Magic itself isn't good or bad. It's all about how you use it and what you want it to do."

"And you think they're using it to try and steal something out of a specific safety deposit box."

"Yes."

"And you know all of this, because you got into some legal trouble in your youth?"

"Because I'm like them," I said. The moment the words left my mouth, I knew he wasn't going to really believe me until he saw proof. Doing it in public didn't thrill me, but the rest of the patrons seemed occupied with their own meals and the servers were busy chatting by the door to the kitchen. "Look, I'll prove it to you."

I let go of the tight leash I'd developed in recent months, giving my magic the chance to do what it wanted while also feeding it my intent to turn my hand translucent. I kept it hidden beyond the computer so no one walking by would see.

His eyes hadn't bugged out when I'd told him magic was real, but they sure as hell did when he saw my hand disappear up to the wrist. The fork he'd been twirling clattered to his plate as he reached out and tried to touch me.

"It's just … gone," he hissed.

"No, it's still there. But the magic alters my skin and muscle and bones at a molecular level to disperse them differently. It makes it appear like it's not there and it lets me pass through solid matter." I demonstrated by putting my hand through the laptop screen and out the other side, letting my fingers grow momentarily solid on the other end.

"Holy shit," he breathed.

"I told you that you'd think I was crazy," I said.

"No. I mean, the idea of magic seems kind of far-fetched and well, impossible. But that, I can't deny what I just saw, and I don't have any other way of explaining it. It would actually explain how they're getting in and out."

"They've also got a lookout, too. I almost caught one of them at the last robbery, but she got away."

"But she was invisible. How could you see her?"

I should have seen this coming. I had been psyching myself up for him not to believe me. I hadn't considered the barrage of questions he'd have about all the mechanics of how magic works.

"Sometimes, people with a lot of power can see or sense other magic being used. Admittedly, I'm not that good at it. But I was able to sense her spell and started to unravel it. Think of it like pulling a loose thread on a sweater."

"What else can you do with it? I mean, can you fly?"

I snorted. "I haven't met anyone who's mastered that ability yet. Sometimes, I can sort of teleport. It's not like what you see in movies. But I can alter the speed at which my body moves in comparison to the world around me and it makes distances a lot shorter. It's actually kind of cool." I sat back and smiled. "I've heard of guys who can create fire."

"So, if I'm understanding this right, it's all done on a molecular level, changing how atoms interact. So, magic is just science we can't see yet?"

"It's a little more complex than that. Not everyone has the capacity to wield magic. It's genetic and runs in the maternal bloodline. It's hardwired into our DNA."

Although that hadn't stopped crazy jackasses from trying to steal it from innocent people. Lucky for them and the rest of the magical community, we'd had a Savior to protect them. I was no Savior, and yet, I was still determined to protect the people of this city.

"That's really fascinating. Have you always been able to turn yourself invisible on command?"

I picked up the napkin tucked under my plate, twisting it into a tight rope to occupy my hands. "That's kind of the part of my past that's not so great. See, magic feeds off our intent. You intend to help an old lady across the street, and suddenly stuff around you stops so you can get her there. You want to rob a bank; it's going to respond with a way to help you do that. The more your intent gets twisted or wrapped up in emotions, the bigger chance it could rebound on you."

"And I'm guessing that's what happened to you?"

"Let's just say I didn't have the greatest childhood and my parents, well my mom especially, was overly concerned with personal safety and security. That led to me doing a lot of spells to stay out of sight. Sneaking out after curfew, things like that. Well, eventually the repeated nature of all that magic got to be too much and it decided it was time to make it permanent."

"I'm sorry. That sounds terrifying. Were you able to talk to anyone about it?"

"Like I said, I fell in with the wrong crowd. They helped me understand what my magic had done and how I could still use it. But it wasn't until I crossed paths with someone who helped me see that I could still use my magic for good. He helped me accept that I still had control over my magic, even when it felt like I was at its mercy."

"For the record, I'm glad you told me. I know we've only known each other for like twenty-four hours, but if I'm being honest, you were kind of a mystery."

I couldn't stop myself from chuckling. "You want to return the favor? I mean, it seems a bit silly I didn't know your first name until just now."

"Oh, I'm an open book. But nothing in my history is nearly as noteworthy as yours."

"Maybe once this case is over you could

give me the highlights, over a drink or something?" I said in a rushed tone.

"I'd like that. Although, I'd be lying if I said I wasn't worried about you being on the rebound."

"Oh, I didn't mean it like that. Just, you know, a friendly drink," I countered. I hadn't meant for it to come out sounding like I was asking him on a date.

It was his turn to look slightly embarrassed. He rubbed the stubble on his chin. "I didn't mean to offend you."

"You didn't. it's totally fine," I said, desperate to change the subject.

He cleared his throat. "So, how'd you break the news to Cartwright and DeWitt?"

"I didn't. Jacquie's former partner was a witch and she brought them both into the fold."

"And I'm guessing it isn't something you just go around telling everyone?"

"Not if I can help it." Heat crept up the nape of my neck. "I may have inadvertently done it with Corbin earlier, trying to get him to open up on our trip to lock-up. But it's pretty clear he's mundane. So, whoever is running the show knows about magic and what it can do, and is using both sides to do their bidding." We still hadn't discussed how Kevin fit in to my hunch and it seemed talking about magic had diverted Duncan's attention.

"So, not to change the subject, but I still don't get how your ex fits in with everything," he said after taking a long sip from his coffee mug.

What, is he a mind reader now?

I took my own fortifying sip of caffeine. "Well, I told you he did time. I was hoping he might have heard something about how our guy's been recruiting practitioners."

"He knows about it, too?"

"Until a few years ago, he had it."

Duncan's face paled. "It's something you can lose?'

"Usually, no. But in some circumstances yeah it can happen. Honestly, I think it saved his life in a way and condemned him to an unfair fate, too."

"Well, do you think that meeting he was attending is over? Our clock is ticking."

I hadn't noticed the time on the sign, but I had to assume J.T. wouldn't hold any meeting longer than an hour. I checked my phone's lock screen. It had been almost that long since we'd left headquarters. After grabbing a stray menu from the table behind us to get the address, I sent Kevin a text with the location, telling him to come as soon as possible.

Please don't let my hopes be for nothing.

THIRTEEN

We'd lapsed into silence after about twenty minutes waiting on Kevin. I downed the rest of my food and our server came by to refill our mugs then take our empty plates away.

"I'm really glad you didn't completely freak out on me," I blurted, drawing Duncan's attention from the laptop screen.

"Oh, don't mistake this cool and collected look for being unaffected. I'm still trying to wrap my head around everything. And if I'm being honest, I'm feeling a little behind the curve, here. I mean, you can literally defy the laws of physics. How do I compete with that?"

I didn't have a chance to answer before the door to the diner opened and Kevin walked in. I turned just in time to see him give a wave to J.T. sitting in a car outside in the parking lot. Kevin spotted us and I immediately moved so he had a place to sit.

"How was your group?" Better to ease into things; show I could still be supportive even if he had blindsided me by dumping me.

He eyed Duncan across the table as the server came by with an empty coffee cup and held up a pot of coffee. Kevin nodded and she poured it before disappearing again.

"It was actually really good to find people who can understand what I've been through," he said.

"He knows about everything," I said.

Kevin turned so quickly in the seat I thought he was going to manage a complete three-sixty. "Since when?"

"Since about an hour ago," I replied. "Look, it's fine. It helps actually. It means I can be honest about what we're facing and how to handle the threat."

"I never thought I'd see the day Kayla Rogers trusted a stranger with her secrets," Kevin murmured. "Maybe I'm not the only one who needs to figure out where they fit in things."

"Can we not do this now? I asked you here, because we need your help."

"I'm here aren't I?" he sighed and downed his cup of coffee in two swigs.

"So, I have a theory that I'm hoping you might be able to help me test out," I began. "We're chasing a robbery crew that is recruiting mundane ex-cons to at least be the front man of the crime, but they're recruiting practitioners to break into the bank's security deposit boxes. If they're finding part of their crew in recently paroled prisoners, why not all of it?"

"You think people talk about our ... gifts inside?" Kevin hissed.

Apparently, my newfound openness about magic wasn't contagious. "Well, yeah. Come on, you can't tell me people like us don't end up behind bars and then brag about it."

Kevin's fingers wrapped around the empty mug in front of him. He wouldn't meet Duncan's gaze and when I tried to catch his eye, he looked past me out the window. Part of me knew it was unfair to use his experience like this. Despite that there was another piece of me that needed to use every available resource I had to ensure people didn't get hurt.

"Come on, Kay, you know I spent a lot of time out of general population," he replied.

"When you first got there, yes. But you were mixing and mingling a lot recently. Anything you heard that might give a hint?"

He shook his head. "Nothing comes to mind. And it wasn't like I went around telling people I knew about magic when I couldn't defend myself once they found out I didn't have any."

It wasn't what I'd hoped to hear. Still I wasn't willing to give up on this thread just yet. Maybe I hadn't pulled at it enough to unravel what was really going on.

"If I wanted to know about magic going on in there, who would I talk to?"

"I just got out. You really think those guys couldn't figure out a way to find me again?"

"There is no way they'd know it was you. There are tons of magical people out there. We could have traced it from any of them," I answered.

"And I'm pretty sure none of them are stupid enough to try and assault a federal agent," Duncan offered.

I wasn't willing to go that far, but he did have a point. The badge I now wore gave me a different level of protection than if I'd just been coming in off the street. But it also made me a target. Either way, I wasn't without my own magical defenses, too.

"Kevin, please, if you can think of anyone that might be able to point us in the right direction, you would be helping more than you know. I swear, after this you don't ever have to see me again." Out of pure habit, my hand closest to him reached for his, going translucent as our fingers touched.

I expected him to pull away. After all, we weren't a couple. I had no right to make such a public show of affection toward him anymore. Yet, he turned his hand over, so our fingers laced together and my hand regained its solidity. "There's one guy who might know what's going on with magic in the prison. His name is Nicholas Kirkland."

Across the table, Duncan began typing, no doubt looking up Mr. Kirkland in the federal database. I waited, sitting there with my hand still pressed into Kevin's until Duncan gave an audible gulp.

"Yeah, I'm starting to think not knowing about magic was better. This guy has a serious sheet. Drugs, sexual assault, attempted murder. Knowing he's got powers just makes this so much worse."

"He definitely scares the shit out of most of the guards and a lot of the inmates give him a wide berth. I can't say that I ever witnessed him do magic while I was there, but he would throw around stories whenever new guys came in. At the time I assumed he was just trying to assert his dominance in the hierarchy, but yeah, I'm not so sure now."

It was a lead we didn't have an hour ago. Now we had two people to follow up on—Kirkland and Corbin's sister. It felt like we were inching along at a snail's pace, but it was at least forward momentum.

"I'll give the prison a call and let them know we're going to be dropping by for a little chat with Mr. Kirkland," Duncan said, getting up and stepping away from the table, phone pressed to his ear.

"So, new partner, huh?" Kevin said, pulling his hand free.

"We've only worked together a couple days."

"And you told him all about magic? You really sure he can be trusted?"

He didn't have to name drop the bastard who'd been the reason Kevin had spent the last two years in prison. I absolutely understood his wariness, but I also knew Ezri had felt that same trepidation and she'd gotten over it, bringing in the people she was working with. It had proved to be life-saving on more than one occasion.

"If it makes you feel any better, my boss told me to do it," I said.

"It's just dangerous and I thought you of all people would get that."

"I'm sorry, you lost the right to have an opinion on that when you broke up with me," I snapped, anger flowing to the surface. "And if something does happen, it's on me, not you."

"I didn't mean ..." he trailed off just as Duncan came back to the table.

"The warden is going to call me back," he said.

"Did you tell him you were with the FBI, and it was related to an ongoing investigation?"

"I got the feeling something was going on with our prisoner and the warden didn't want to share details."

Great.

That put a damper on our plans to dig into what Kirkland knew. We still had Corbin's sister to follow up.

"Even if we can't get in to see him right away, we do have that other stop to make," I addressed Duncan.

"Right."

I turned to Kevin. "Can we drop you somewhere? Your mom's place?"

"No, I've got a ride," he answered and gestured out the window again.

I turned to find J.T. still sitting in his car. I could see him staring at his phone. I hadn't realized he was Kevin's ride. He was really taking his responsibility of being a support and mentor to the magical community seriously. Then again, when your wife had been the Savior of the whole magical community, it's hard not to want to live up to that expectation.

"Good," I said, trying not to feel the sea of emotions warring inside me in this moment.

"I hope you find what you're looking for, Kay," he said before standing up. He held out a hand to Duncan. "Nice to meet you, Agent. Take good care of her."

"Thanks for your help," Duncan answered and shook his hand.

We both watched Kevin leave the diner. My heart hammered for a moment against my ribcage. I hadn't expected my two worlds to collide like this. For the briefest of moments, I couldn't help wondering if Ezri had felt like this on her first case. She'd acted tough when we first met and stubborn as hell. Yet I had to assume she'd struggled, too. A pang of sadness squeezed my lungs as the realization hit me again that I couldn't' share the person I was becoming with her, who I was becoming thanks to her.

"We should get going," Duncan announced, closing the laptop and tucking it beneath his arm. "I'll update the boss on the way. I think your instincts are right. It's time we go find Corbin's sister and see what she knows."

FOURTEEN

We reached the car just as my phone buzzed with an incoming call from Molly. I climbed into the passenger seat and answered, as Duncan wedged the laptop between his body and the steering column to presumably do a search for Corbin's sister's last known address.

"Checking up on me, boss?" I asked.

"Kind of in the job description," she answered. "How'd it go?"

"Uh, well Avery's doing her thing and will let us know if she can get anything usable off the footage. And we think we might have a lead on what is motivating Corbin to keep his mouth shut."

"Such as?" she prodded.

"He's got a sister. The last time he got arrested and did time, it was for assaulting her abusive boyfriend."

"Worth a dig for sure."

"I might have another angle I'm working about our lookouts."

"Keep us apprised," Molly replied. A pause and then, "... Did you think about that other thing we discussed?"

"Actually, I did. And I realized given everything that's going on with this case, I didn't have any way to explain my theories without admitting the truth."

"Did you know she can put her hand through computers?" Duncan offered cheerily, his voice loud enough to carry over the line.

"Sounds like it wasn't a disaster," Molly noted.

"The coffee and breakfast might have had something to do with it."

Molly burst into laughter on the other end of the line. I waited for it to subside, but it appeared she couldn't catch her breath.

"I didn't think it was that hilarious," I muttered.

"S-sorry," Molly gasped, finally getting herself under control. "It's just, after Ezri exposed me to magic, she took me to some dive diner to answer all of my questions. I guess *that's kind of a tradition or something.*"

Or something.

"We also have another lead we're working on following, too. Thanks to Kevin."

"That must have been awkward, I'm sorry."

"It's fine," I said through pursed lips.

"I've got an address," Duncan announced, interrupting the conversation.

I gave him a thumbs up as he input the address in the GPS and stowed the laptop in the back seat. "I'll keep you apprised," I said and ended the call.

"So, when we get there, how do we want to play it?" Duncan asked as he pulled out of the diner's lot and onto the highway heading into the city.

"I mean, we can let her know her brother's been arrested for robbing a bank and see what comes of it. Name drop Kirkman and see if that sticks. I'd really like to know if she visited him regularly while he was locked up."

"Add it to the list of things to figure out when we head back to the prison," he noted.

We lapsed into silence as I watched traffic whiz by. Thanks to our brunch, there weren't as many cars on the road and we made it to Corbin's sister's apartment in Dorchester before noon. We pulled into an empty space by the building and Duncan cut the engine.

"What if she's not home?" I said, putting voice to the fear that whispered in the back of my mind.

Duncan's cheeks flushed and he rubbed at his brow. "I, uh, hadn't thought about that."

"Did your digging show anything about where she might work? I mean, if there was an abusive relationship maybe she had to file a temporary restraining order keeping him away from her at home and work?"

He looked at me and smiled in that shy way of his. "Good thing I've got you backing me up."

I retrieved the laptop he'd been using and scoured the state's court system databases. It didn't take long to find that she had such an order in place for the last nine months. "Bingo. Work address," I said proudly.

"Maybe she's taking a sick day," he said and climbed out of the car.

I trailed him up to the second floor to the apartment all the way at the end of the hallway. I knocked sharply twice, "Christina Wayne," I called.

The door to the next apartment opened and an elderly man stuck his head out, tufts of greying hair shooting out of his head with a prominent bald patch on top. "She's not here."

I turned to address the man, making sure he could see my badge. "Does she usually work now?"

His gaze narrowed. "Let me see that badge."

I closed the distance and held it out for him to examine. "She's not in trouble. We just wanted to ask her some questions," I explained.

"She's a nice girl. Happier since she kicked that piece of trash boyfriend out. Yeah, she mentioned she was working a double today and to feed her cat tonight."

"Thank you for your help."

We retraced our steps back to the car and headed for what turned out to be a small convenience store tucked in between a yoga studio and a nail salon. Duncan reached for the door when I stopped him.

"My gut tells me she doesn't really trust many men. Maybe it's better I try talking to her on my own," I said.

He released his grip on the door handle. "I'll check in with the warden and see what's going on with Kirkland."

Stepping into the tiny store sent shivers down my spine. Not from nerves, but since the air conditioning was on high blast. The woman behind the counter sat draped in a fuzzy shawl. She wore a name tag bearing the name Chrissy on it.

"Can I help you with something?" Her voice was hoarse.

"I'm looking for Christina Wayne," I replied.

Her posture stiffened and both hands found the edge of the counter. "Who are you?"

"Christina, my name is Special Agent Kayla Rogers. I was hoping I could talk to you about your brother, Corbin."

The stiffness in her shoulders sagged instantly. "What's he done now?"

"He's been arrested for robbing a bank. He was apprehended on scene, and didn't do anything to conceal his identity."

"No, that's not true. My brother has his issues, but no, he'd never do something that stupid."

"We know he's working with someone, but he's been reluctant to share details. We think he might be trying to protect someone." I leaned in closer. "You."

"Look, I love my brother and I know he can be a mess. But he swore to me he was done with being the overprotective big brother."

"I've read the reports on his last arrest. It sounds like he did you a favor."

"Yes, Jesse was an awful prick. I begged the cops not to arrest Corbin, but I don't know anything about a bank robbery."

"He'd recently been paroled, right?"

"Yeah. But he got out early for good behavior."

"And yet, he went and did something that landed him right back in prison. Doesn't seem like the kind of move someone would make unless they were under duress." I took a breath. "Are you sure you haven't noticed anyone strange following you or people paying you more attention?"

Color drained from her face. "I thought I was just being paranoid. But the last couple of days, maybe a week, I could swear I felt someone watching me. But no one was ever there."

Not that you could see.

"Did you notice it anywhere in particular? Here or at home?"

"Mostly here. Part of me thought Jesse was trying to get back at me, but he's never been afraid to show his face. I'm honestly surprised the court order has stopped him from coming around."

"Thank you." I handed her my card. "If you can think of anything else, please call me."

I found Duncan waiting by the car. "She thinks someone's been watching her."

"Did she give a description?"

"No, because she said every time she looked there was no one there."

"Do you think it's someone using *magic*?" He whispered the last word.

"Only one way to tell," I said and blew out a breath.

Sensing other magic was never my strength, but I had to try. "Okay, look, I'm about to do something and it's going to look like I'm doing nothing. But I need you to stay still and not talk," I explained.

"Sure thing."

I closed my eyes, letting the world fall away one sense at a time. Taste was always the easiest to ignore, followed shortly by touch, and with my eyes closed, sight was temporarily blocked. Wrangling my other senses would allow for that to be stronger when the time came. Only sound and smell were stronger now. I didn't need to smell for what I was planning and did my best to focus only on enhancing my hearing. I reached for my magic, teasing it from its light slumber.

I need you now.

Lavender infused every fiber of my being, eager to do my bidding. The world around me thrummed with power, too. I wasn't the world's strongest witch by any stretch of the imagination, but I could still draw on the world's magic when my intent and need were strong enough. I don't think I ever truly appreciated the way natural magic felt when it boosted my own spells. It was like a tangible thing, bumping against me, latching tight to my body.

The ambient voices of passersby crashed over me, like they were shouting at me from close proximity through a bullhorn. *Too much focus*. The magic around me softened and the sounds decreased in volume. I tried to focus on sounds that might signal someone's weight shifting in place. The rustle of fabric as they moved. The nearest sounds to hit me came directly from behind me. I had to assume that Duncan was watching me work.

Blocking him out, I did my best to search down the street. I turned in the direction I thought would have the better vantage point of the convenience store. Something clattered in the distance, and I opened my eyes. My own power sharpened my vision, and I studied the empty patch of sidewalk under a pale blue awning. It appeared to be an empty space except for the shape of a cell phone lying on the ground. A cell phone that was mysteriously hovering into the air.

"Stay here," I told Duncan.

I leapt into the street without looking, letting the magic around push me forward like a gust of wind. I was already across the street before the first car went whizzing past behind me. All I could see was the cell phone still hovering in midair. I held out a hand and could feel this practitioner's magic bump up against my own much like the lookout had done at the bank yesterday. My fingers were nimbler this time as I found the edges of the spell and put out one simple word into the world.

Unravel.

With an almost audible 'pop' the magic disappeared, revealing a young woman standing before me. She wore a hoodie and dark glasses, but I was almost certain she'd been the lookout from yesterday.

"It's impolite to stalk people while invisible," I said and clamped a hand down on her wrist before she pulled another vanishing act. "I'm with the FBI."

If I had to, I'd find a way to literally bind us together to keep her from taking off. I dragged her back across the street to where Duncan stood. His jaw was slack as he took in what had just happened.

"Yeah, that's going to take some getting used to," he murmured.

"Why don't we start with your name?" I prompted.

"Go to hell," she spat.

I could see the top of a slender wallet protruding from her hoodie pocket and held out a hand. She glared at me and pulled against my grip. I didn't need her to cooperate. It was enough for me to just want to see her ID for it to zip out of her pocket and into my hand.

"Serena Beck from Mattapan," I said, checking the photo on the ID to her. They matched. I skimmed the other information on the ID. She was just twenty years old.

"How about you tell us why you've been watching that woman, Serena?" I said, putting myself between our stalker and the brick façade of the convenience store.

"I wasn't do anything," she answered.

My grip was such that I could push up the sleeve of her hoodie to reveal the branded mark of the Order—a scythe and triple spiral. It turned my stomach.

"I know you and I crossed paths yesterday. And I have a sneaking suspicion you were about to text your boss about us," I replied, plucking the phone from her hands and passing it to Duncan.

"We're going to take a little ride," I said and ushered her into the back seat of the car.

Duncan stepped around me, pulling out his phone and pressed the pads of her fingers to the touch screen. The laptop offered up a helpful ping when it bounced back her police record—mostly arrests for loitering and one for underage drinking. Nothing that would connect her to Corbin or Kirkland. She hadn't ever done time, but it appeared she had been on probation for the underage drinking charges.

I took Serena's phone, but found it locked and only accessible by a fingerprint. I had no doubt Serena would refuse to help, but I turned to look at her anyway, holding the device aloft. "You feel like unlocking this for us?"

"Fuck you."

I'd been nice so far. I wasn't sure I was going to be able to accomplish what I had in mind. Avery would have known exactly what to do, but I couldn't run to her every time I had a problem that needed solving. Not if I was going to prove myself, that I could do this job. So, I pressed one hand to the laptop screen that was displaying her fingerprint card and pressed my right index finger to the button on the phone. The scent of lavender rose up around me and I could feel a prickling sensation on the pad of my finger. Almost like that part of my hand had just fallen asleep, and it was just now waking. The lock screen vanished, revealing the factory default home screen.

"Uh, how did you do that?" Duncan whispered.

"Probably better you don't know right now," I replied. I went into the settings and disabled the lock screen altogether.

"We need to get back to headquarters and drop her off before our next stop," I noted.

"You really have no idea what you're

dealing with," Serena piped up from the back seat as we left the convenience store and Christina behind.

I had no doubt she would try to talk her way out of whatever we were going to throw at her. And really, what could we charge her with? Technically, she was right. All I'd seen her doing was standing on a sidewalk with a cell phone and that wasn't a crime. Even if my superiors understood the ramifications of magic and how it intersected with crime, that didn't mean a judge or a prosecutor would understand that she'd been using magic to conceal herself to spy on an innocent woman.

"There's still time for you to help us, Serena. Tell us what you know. Maybe we can help you out, too," I offered, turning to face the young woman.

She crossed her arms over her chest and turned her gaze out the window. That was fine. I could use the trip back downtown to start sifting through her phone. At least, that's what I would have done if my own phone hadn't started ringing.

"Rogers," I answered on the second ring.

"Where are you and Duncan?" Jacquie's voice was strained.

"Just on our way back to headquarters. What's wrong? Has there been another robbery?"

"No. Corbin Wayne was attacked in the prison. He's in the infirmary. It looks pretty bad."

Shit.

"We've got a potential witness. We'll drop them off at headquarters and then head over to the prison to interview him."

"Something tells me this isn't what Corbin expected when he took the fall," she said.

No, I doubted he thought he would end up lying in a prison infirmary. I ended the call and filled Duncan in as he pulled into the employee lot at headquarters. I turned again to survey Serena.

"I'm going to trust that you aren't going to go walking through walls."

"You have nothing I want," she said, but didn't fight as Duncan escorted her inside.

I waited for him to return, but fifteen minutes later I spotted Jacquie walking toward the car. She took up residence behind the wheel and put the car into drive before I could ask about the partner switch.

"Do we know anything about who attacked Corbin?" I had a hunch about who it might be, but I hadn't gotten a chance to share that information with either her or Molly yet.

"All I know is the warden called to tell us Corbin had ended up in the infirmary."

"Did he mention anything about another inmate named Kirkman?"

"No. He wasn't exactly forthcoming with details. Why, who is Kirkman?"

"Kevin said he's the go-to guy for magical information behind bars. Brutal thug of a guy."

"But you said that Corbin wasn't magical. Why would someone with power care about him?"

"I don't know. Maybe he's part of the pipeline for our ringleader? We were hoping to get a face to face with him, but the warden ghosted us."

Now, it seemed maybe the warden had a good reason. If he had inmates trying to kill each other, that would put a damper on getting back to the FBI, no matter how high and mighty we saw ourselves. That still didn't mean it didn't frustrate the fuck out of me.

"I recognize that look," Jacquie said softly.

"What look?" I replied.

"The 'there's got to be a magical solution to this problem, but it's not coming to me' look. Ezri used to get it sometimes. I don't think she even noticed she did it."

Yet another thing we shared that I hadn't anticipated. "I know it's stupid to try and think I'm filling her shoes or replacing her, but Molly told me that Ezri broke the news about all of this in a diner. And I literally just did that with Duncan."

"She was your motivation to take up this fight. It's natural she's going to be on your mind, especially on your first case. But, believe me, you wouldn't have been top of your class if you didn't deserve to be here, doing the work. You need to trust your instincts."

"My instincts feel like they're leading me in circles."

"Or maybe they're zeroing in on what's really important," she replied as the prison gates coming into view.

One of us was about to be proven right.

FIFTEEN

I braced myself as a stony-faced guard led us to the infirmary. The room was sparsely populated with a pulled curtain around a bed at the far end of the ward that signaled our destination. Our guide stood sentinel on the outside of the curtain as I pushed it aside and stepped through.

"Damn," I hissed as I took in the sight of Corbin's bloodied face.

I noted dark bruises around his throat, and spotted the edges of bandages poking out from beneath his prison jumpsuit. Someone had definitely done a number on him. His right eye was swollen shut, but his left fluttered open and he turned to look at us.

"No, not you," he groaned, doing the best he could to pull away from me while being handcuffed to the bed.

Given the state of his injuries that seemed an unnecessary cruelty. I stepped up and pressed a finger to the cuff around his wrist. I felt the metal give way beneath my touch, destabilizing until it sat reformed on the bed beside him. He lifted his hand as if seeing it for the first time.

"You look like you're in enough pain as it is," I said and leaned down. "How about it's our little secret?"

He massaged his wrist and swallowed, his Adam's apple bobbing prominently in his throat. I could hear the discomfort as he swallowed. "What do you want?"

"Well, for starters, it would be helpful if you could tell us what happened."

"Nothing," he said, shrinking back against the pillow.

Beside me, Jacquie disappeared through

the curtain, returning a moment later with a chair. I took a seat at Corbin's bedside. "Chrissy is safe. I swear to you, she's okay."

He blinked at me through his good eye. "How …"

"I understand why you want to protect her. Family can be all we have in this world. But you don't need to protect the person who hired you, because they clearly don't care about you. Please, Corbin, let me help you."

He turned his head away from me and I could feel my frustration bubbling to the surface. I looked over at Jacquie who stood off to one side, taking in the scene. I both wanted her to jump in and guide the conversation, and to remain silent so I could work through this on my own.

"Look, I get that you don't trust me and that I freaked you out. I'm honestly sorry about that, okay. I thought you knew what was going on and I was wrong. But that doesn't mean we can't help each other out. Cooperate with us and I know we can put in a good word with the prosecutor. Maybe you'll even be able to see your sister without Plexiglass between you sooner than you think."

"Look, I don't even know the guys who jumped me. But they said it was a message from some guy I'd never heard of before," he said, still refusing to look at me.

"Kirkland?" I filled in. My voice carried a hopeful note.

Corbin's head whipped back around, and he regarded me with fear plastered on his face. He opened his mouth, but no words came out. It was all the confirmation I needed.

"Did they say anything else about why he wanted you jumped?"

"No," he rasped.

There was more to the story than he was letting on. Though I was honestly surprised he'd given me that much. There were other ways of getting that sort of information.

"Thank you. Rest up," I said and reached for the handcuff. He gave me a plaintive look with his good eye, but I couldn't explain how I'd managed to uncuff him without the keys. "Sorry."

The cuff went immaterial in my fingers as I slid it back around his wrist. I did manage to loosen it by one click and I heard him give an audible sigh when his hand hit the bed.

"I think we need to have a chat with the warden," I told Jacquie as a different guard escorted us out of the infirmary.

"He's not the only one," Jacquie replied.

I WAS PREPARED to give the warden a piece of my mind for blowing Duncan off until I walked into his office to find him mopping sweat from his brow and looking like he might be sick. I'd never met the man in the time I'd been coming to visit Kevin.

"You're here about Corbin Wayne, I presume," he said, clearing his throat.

"And Nicholas Kirkland," I replied. "We have reason to believe he's behind Mr. Wayne's assault."

"I don't know what that boy told you, but

Kirkland was nowhere near the scene when guards broke it up."

"That doesn't mean he didn't orchestrate the attack," Jacquie replied coolly. "And independent of the assault, we have reason to speak with him regarding an ongoing investigation."

"He's been in solitary the last two weeks."

"Well, it's time to get him out," I snapped then planted my feet and crossed my arms over my chest. "We'll wait."

The warden held up his hands in a placating gesture. "All right. It's going to take me a minute. A guard will come get you when he's been brought up to the visitation room."

Jacquie spun on her heel without a word and parked herself right outside the warden's office. I joined her. "I think you scared him."

"Not the first time I've had to put a man in his place." After a beat she continued, "I think I should question Kirkland."

"I get that he's a dangerous guy, but I can take care of myself," I protested.

"If he's part of the magical community

and he's seen you visiting Kevin while he was here, it would raise too many questions and could put Kevin in danger. That said, I'm not saying you can't be in the room with me."

"But how …?" The question died on my lips.

Why didn't I think of that?

A guard with a stocky build and thick mustache appeared, gesturing for us to follow him. Jaquie made a show of standing first. "Wait here."

I waited until they were out of view before letting my magic wash over me. I hadn't felt this sort of excitement at using my magic this way in a long time. Not since it had first happened and I'd seen what I could do with it, consequences be damned. I sprinted out of the office and fell into step beside Jacquie, nudging her shoulder just enough to let her know I was with her again.

"Please wait outside," Jacquie instructed the guard once we reached a separate visitation room.

"Orders are not to leave the prisoner," the guard answered.

"He's shackled right?" she retorted, and he nodded. "I'll be fine."

The guard looked like he wanted to protest further, but kept his mouth shut. Holding the door open, I waited for Jacquie to step inside first. I could have slipped in behind her before the door closed, but old habits were already kicking in. I simply passed through the closed door and took in the scene before me. Jacquie sat on one side of the table while a muscled man with fists the size of ham hocks sat across from her. He didn't look the least bit bothered by her presence, nor was he intimidated by the glare she gave him.

"I'm Special Agent Jacquie DeWitt," she introduced. "And you're going to tell me why you ordered a hit on a new arrival, Corbin Wayne."

"I'm not telling you anything, bitch," he spat.

I had to stop myself from lashing out at him. Jacquie could handle herself and that wasn't the reason I was in here hidden with magic. I needed to determine if he, too, had power. I moved to stand behind him, letting my sense of touch amplify. The air around me became heavy with the weight of the magic that existed in this place. It felt almost restrained, as if someone had purposely dampened its effects. It made a certain amount of sense. After all, if people with magic landed in here, it would be easy for them to literally pull a disappearing act and jail break without anyone being the wiser.

I held my hands out in front of me, testing to see if my magic bumped against his. It was there, prickly and defensive the moment I even got close. His body jerked at the intrusion, and he turned, his gaze looking right through me.

"You seem jumpy, Mr. Kirkland," Jacquie noted.

"You're wasting your breath. I don't have anything to say to you."

"Oh, come on. I hear you're the big man around here. Nothing happens without your say so," she goaded, leaning back in her chair.

"I didn't lay a hand on him," he spat.

"Well, now that I'd say I believe under normal circumstances, but these aren't normal circumstances." She clasped her hands in front of her. "I've seen your record, Mr. Kirkland. We both know you're not getting out of here any time soon. And even the warden thinks you had something to do with that beat down. Now, you can cooperate and tell me why you would target him and maybe I can help you avoid some extra years to your sentence. Or keep your mouth shut and spend even more time in solitary."

Just knowing this man had magic wasn't enough. My gut told me he'd rather spend the rest of his time here in solitary than nark to a cop. Despite that, we still needed to know what he knew. I knew it was possible to go into people's memories with magic, but I'd never been privy to the nitty-gritty. Still, it wasn't such an uncommon skill that I couldn't figure it out.

I knew physical contact had to be made; of that much I was certain. I just prayed skin-to-skin contact wasn't necessary, because while I may be insubstantial in most ways, I couldn't say that he wouldn't notice a hand on the back of his neck. So, I opted for his shoulder.

Please let this work.

I poured out my intent into the tiny space, willing my magic to keep me hidden while also allowing me to access his memories. Slowly, the room and its occupants slid into fuzzy darkness, replaced by a blank space. That soon resolved into tiny doors. The first I pushed open to find a flurry of thoughts and images of people and places I had no context for. Except I got the distinct feeling that they were Kirkland's memories as a child from the perspective, coupled with the emotions washing over me; nervous energy mixed with confusion and a gnawing need to belong. I stepped away from that door and moved to another. I slammed it shut almost immediately. Even just a brief glimpse told me that's where he kept his memories of the crimes he'd committed. I didn't' need to live through that trauma.

I reached for the next one and what appeared to be a wooden frame rippled, transforming into a steel door with a combination lock. Whatever lay within this room was given the highest security. I bent and studied the tumblers finding letters instead of numbers, with spaces for four digits.

"How the hell am I supposed to figure that out?" I griped before I realized no one could hear me.

"You don't' belong here," Kirkland's voice called behind me.

I spun to find a version of him standing there in a tailored suit, crackling balls of energy bobbing in his hands. Well, shit. I had not anticipated that.

"I don't suppose you'd like to help me open that door, there?" I said, hooking a thumb over my shoulder.

"I don't know how you got in here, but you're going to leave," he howled and lobbed one of his swirling energy balls at my head.

My magic should have responded and deflected the energy, or at the very least turned me incorporeal enough for it to pass through me. It did neither. In fact, it felt almost as though my magic had deserted me. The energy grazed my shoulder, sending searing jolts of pain down my left arm.

"You're on my turf now, bitch," he laughed, readying to send the other one my direction.

This might be his domain, but I *wasn't* powerless, damn it. I positioned myself with the fortified door to my back, ready to dodge his next blow. It came speeding at my head before I could even catch a breath. Except this time, I was just fast enough to avoid it making contact. Instead, it slammed into the door. One of the little tumblers spun, dropping into place, N.

I can't believe that worked.

"That can't be your only trick," I taunted. "Show me what you've got tough guy."

"I wonder, if you die in here, do you die wherever you are?" he sneered, upping the ante by transforming the energy balls into bolts of arcing electricity.

I had no intention of finding out. I threw myself down as the electrical current zipped toward me in the air. It collided with the door and another tumbler dropped, L.

Whatever he was hiding was protected by a four letter word beginning with an N and ending with an L. "How about you just tell me why you went after Corbin Wayne? Did he offend you somehow? Was it tacky of him to get caught? Is that what pissed you off?"

"Couldn't be sure he hadn't talked," Kirkland said.

That was something. I know I hadn't gotten a good look at whoever gave Corbin the phone at Notre Dame, but I was fairly certain they were far skinnier than Kirkland. Plus, as far as I knew, he'd been locked in solitary.

"Well, you made sure he couldn't talk," I said. "Not sure he's even going to survive now."

He flipped me off—rude—and sent another bolt of lightning my way. It struck too high on the door to trigger another tumbler, but I couldn't expect him to do all the heavy lifting. So, I focused, searching for my own magic in this hostile landscape. It was weaker than it should have been, but I was trying to fuel two and very soon three spells simultaneously. That was far more than I'd ever tried before.

I threw up a barrier between us. It shimmered glossy and pale, and it withstood the first barrage of attacks he sent my way. It wouldn't hold for long. I fell to my knees by the door, doing my best to grasp the middle two tumblers and spin them. Logically I knew at least one had to be a vowel. I flipped the first to an A and the second to an I, but the lock didn't budge. I flipped the first spot to an E and the I to an A, but again nothing. I could feel the barrier weakening behind me. It took more concentration than it should have to get my hands to move as I tried the only other combination that made sense. N-O-E-L. Why he would be thinking about a Christmas word made no sense to me, but the lock disappeared and the door vanished.

"No!"

The word tore from Kirkland's throat. It echoed so strangely in my ears, I couldn't be sure if he'd spoken it here in his head or in the visitation room with Jacquie. Could it have been both? The images that flew by made no sense. They were rushing too quickly, and I had no context for them, but I thought I caught sight of a skinny figure with Kirkland. Some of it looked to be from before his stint in prison, while others might have been visitations. I could see their lips moving, but there were no words that I could make out. Not until I picked up on one word.

"Noel."

Not like the Christmas word, more like the name. There was no surname to go along with it, but it was a start. Unfortunately picking up on that single word was enough to divert my attention and the barrier dividing us fizzled out of existence. Kirkland's magical manifestation towered over me; hands outstretched to no doubt snuff me out.

I couldn't let him test that theory about dying in someone else's mind. I gathered the focus I still had and tried to picture myself back in the room with Jaquie. Slowly, too slowly, my surroundings dissolved back into the room where Jacquie sat opposite Kirkland. He had his hands outstretched toward her, like he had held them in his mind. I broke the contact between us, hoping it would be enough to pull him from his own head.

"I gave you the chance to help me. Sorry you didn't take it," Jacquie said as I staggered backwards, my body flitting between visible and incorporeal. I silently prayed the camera wouldn't pick anything up. Jacquie shot me a warning look as she stood and pounded her fist twice on the door. It swung inward and the guard appeared, hauling Kirkland to his feet.

"I can find my way out," Jacquie assured the guard.

I waited a painful count of ten before letting the magic fall away around me. The simple act of releasing the spell was enough to wipe me out. I slumped into the seat Kirkland had just vacated.

"What happened to your arm?" Jacquie whispered.

I glanced at my shoulder and saw the singed fabric and angry red flesh beneath it. I should have realized any injuries I'd sustained there would translate back to the real world. After all, the first time I'd met Ezri, she'd been battered and bleeding from fighting some magical computer virus.

"I'll be fine," I said, trying to put on a brave face. "I got a name."

SIXTEEN

"We need to get you medical attention," Jacquie said as she tugged off her suit jacket and slung it over my shoulder to hide the damage.

"I'll deal with it later," I said, trying to ignore the throbbing pain that was steadily dissipating. That wasn't a good sign.

"No, I'm calling J.T.," she replied as we left the prison behind.

"He's got more important things to do. I can patch myself up," I protested.

"That requires magic," she said pointedly.

I wasn't sure I could conjure enough

power right now to heal a pimple. I hated that she had a point, but I also knew she was right. If I stayed injured, there was no way I'd be able to stay on the case.

"I got a name, Noel," I said as I waited for her to dial J.T.'s number.

"Happen upon a last name?" she asked, setting the phone on the dash.

"No. But I think whoever this guy is, is the same one who I saw in the surveillance video meeting with Corbin. And Kirkland admitted to me that he ordered the hit on Corbin, because he wanted to ensure he hadn't talked."

"Well, you got more out of him than I did. He just sort of stared at me blankly and then started lunging at me."

"His mind was weird. Like a bunch of locked doors, compartmentalizing everything in his life. And the information about this Noel guy was locked behind stronger protection. I got lucky and managed to get it open. But I couldn't make out much of anything that was happening. I think he might have visited Kirkland in prison. We should check visitor logs."

"That's good work."

"I should have remembered that whatever happened to me in there, would manifest here though." My entire left arm was beginning to go numb now.

"She made it look easy, but I know it took more of a toll on her than she cared to admit."

Her phone buzzed on the dash and she scooped it up. "Good, he's going to meet us back at FBI headquarters. Looks like Molly and Duncan might have something from the woman you brought in."

I focused my attention on making sure I kept blood flowing through my left arm, flexing the fingers on my hand to make sure I could still feel something while Jacquie wove through traffic. My head was beginning to swim as the sun started its afternoon descent toward the horizon.

"What the hell happened?" J.T. demanded when he saw the state of my injuries in the parking lot.

"I zigged when I should have zagged," I answered.

The overpowering scent of honey smacked me in the face as he began running his hands up and down my arm. Jacquie gave a fake cough and gestured to the entrance to the building.

"It's better if we do this inside."

Even just a little boost from his magic was enough to take the edge off of my fear that my arm was going to wind up useless. We found Molly and Duncan in the conference room. Serena was nowhere to be seen.

"You're hurt," Duncan proclaimed when I walked in.

"We're working on that," Jacquie said. "We might have a first name of an associate and Kayla thinks it might be our ringleader on the outside."

"At least one of us had some success," Molly sighed. "Your girl isn't talking. Even when I told her we would protect her."

J.T. ushered me to a chair at the end of the table and went back to tending to my arm. The room swam in and out of focus as the numbness in my extremity subsided, replaced by burning hot pins and needles. I bit down hard on my tongue to keep from screaming as the pain washed over me, bringing with it a bout of nausea.

"I'd tell you to rest for a few days to let the healing process really kick in, but I'm not stupid enough to think you're not going right back out there," J.T. told me, his voice low.

"We're close to breaking this case. I can feel it."

"She used to get like that, too. And as much as I wanted to tether her to a bed to keep her safe, I knew it wasn't worth the frustration on my part."

"If Noel is a criminal connection, he's not showing up in any of the databases," Duncan announced, pulling my attention from J.T. and the soothing touch of his magic.

"I have to believe whoever he is; he wouldn't be stupid enough to use a real name on the visitor logs," Jacquie said. "Especially if he knew he was going to be robbing banks."

"Hey, do me a favor and pull up Kirkland's file again," I said, addressing Duncan.

I pushed my chair around the edge of the table and pulled myself to sit beside him. He passed the laptop over and I scrolled through the file until I got to the end where it showed images of his distinguishing marks and tattoos. There it was on his left bicep—the scythe and triple spiral. He was an Order member. That could explain why Serena had been involved. Maybe she wasn't as scared as she'd been letting on. There was only one way to find out.

"I'm going to talk to Serena," I said, and was on my feet before anyone could protest.

Molly grabbed my uninjured arm long enough to spin me and aim in the right direction. I found Serena sitting in one of the smaller offices, hands clasped in her lap, head bowed. Almost like she was praying. I don't think I was the savior she was asking for.

"Tell me what drew you to the Order," I said bluntly.

Her head whipped up and she stared at me, mouth agape like a fish caught on a line. "I don't ..."

"Don't bullshit me, Serena." I grabbed her wrist and shoved up the sleeve of her hoodie. "It's a very distinctive brand. I know your buddy Nicholas Kirkland's got one, too."

"That guy is insane," she said, yanking her wrist away from me. "And I'm not involved. They don't actually exist anymore."

"They don't have coherent leadership, but the people who believed in their cause are still out there. You looking to make a name for yourself?"

"No. Look, I was angry when this happened," she said and gestured to herself, "and they seemed like they could help me figure it out. I didn't want anything to do with their anarchist shit."

For a split second, I could see a younger version of myself sitting there saying the same thing. I hadn't managed to get wrapped up in the Order in my youth, but I had probably came closer than I ever realized.

"I get that more than you can possibly know," I said, taking on a gentler tone.

"Right, because a Fed gets me," she spat defensively.

"I do. Believe it or not, I used to be a lot like you, Serena. In fact, the entire reason I'm working on this case is because I used to be wrapped up in this stuff."

She studied me in silence for a minute before speaking. "You're like me?"

"Guilty as charged. But there's people who can help you learn to use your magic for good, to help people. It doesn't have to control you anymore. They don't have to control you."

"What would I have to do?"

"Just tell me what you know."

"I just watched when that guy you arrested went into the bank. I didn't know what he was doing. I was told to just stay unseen and if things went bad, I was supposed to tell Ronnie to get out."

"Is Ronnie the one who went into the vault?"

She nodded wordlessly.

"Do you know what they're looking for? Was this the only time you were involved?"

Tears sparkled in her eyes. "All I know is, we'd know it when we find it. It's magical and it's supposed to be highly valuable."

"What about the other banks?'

"Yeah, I was there."

"Was Ronnie the one going into the vault then, too?"

She shook her head. "Different people each time."

"Did you recruit them or did the person running the show pick them out?"

The tears that had been shining in her eyes now trickled down her cheeks, leaving tiny rivulets on her skin. "He told me I had to bring them or else he'd make sure I ended up in prison."

"Is his name Noel?"

She shrunk back from me, as if I'd slapped her. That had struck a nerve. Now we were getting somewhere. I had to assume Serena was getting the other Whisperers from that group my mom had mentioned. For the span of a few heartbeats, I feared she'd get roped into it, just to prove she could help me and that I needed her back in my life.

"Who is he, Serena?"

"You can't protect me."

"We can try. But we need to know what we're up against. You have your whole life ahead of you. Don't let this define you."

She wiped her cheeks with the backs of her hands. "A few months ago, I got probation. Stupid drinking thing." I already knew that. "Even though I didn't get locked up, I still have a probation officer. At first, I thought it wasn't so bad. I feel better when I'm not drinking. So, the meetings really helped. But then everything changed."

"Where did you meet Noel?"

"He's my probation officer," she whispered.

That explained why he didn't show up on the criminal offender databases. He was working on our side of the law. "Did he know you had magic?"

"I don't know how he did, because I never told him. But one day, I went to check in with him and he told me that he knew I could do things that most people would believe was impossible. And he wanted me to show him."

"Had he tried to do anything else?"

"No. Nothing like that. But once he knew what I could do and that there were other people like me out there, he started holding my freedom over me. And then a few weeks ago, he came to me and told me that I had to show up at an address and bring another Whisperer with me."

"You said he let you pick the people."

"He made me give him names of people who I knew. More of them had criminal records than I realized, because he started to give me a list of people I had to pick from. He said if they didn't agree, he'd find a way to make their lives hell."

A plan was already taking shape in my mind as she talked. It was dangerous and I wasn't sure my magic would cooperate, but it was all I had. I reached out and gave Serena's hands a squeeze. "Wait here. I'll be back."

"Where are you going?'

"I'm going to make sure he never hurts anyone ever again."

THE CONFERENCE ROOM was quiet when I walked back in. J.T. had left, and Molly and Jacquie stood off to one side as Duncan studied something on the laptop in front of him.

"We're looking in the wrong place," I announced.

"What'd she tell you?" Jacquie asked.

"That Noel is her probation officer, and he is threatening to violate the terms of her probation if she doesn't cooperate with his scheme. He's forcing her to recruit other Whisperers with criminal pasts. She was involved in all of the robberies as the lookout."

"Your freelancer friend just sent over some information on the footage we gave her. Looks like we might have some more names to run by Serena," Duncan said.

"Good." I started pacing the short distance from the door to the far wall. "I don't know if this guy has magic himself or if he is just in the know, but he brought it up unprompted with Serena."

"I think the warden was jarred by your visit earlier, because he just sent over the visitor logs for Kirkland from the last six months," Molly interjected.

Duncan pulled up the digital log. Nothing stood out other than I was surprised a man capable of such violence had any visitors at all. I was about to pronounce the log a bust when I spotted a pattern. Every week for the last four months, he'd had consistent visits from a Leon Winters.

"Duncan, check for any probation or parole officers by the name of Noel Winters."

"Nothing," he replied, but then tapped a few more keys. "But I do have a Noel Verano."

"Let me see what he looks like," I prodded, and he brought up a photo likely used for his work ID.

I couldn't be sure, but he looked like the

right build for the man I'd glimpsed in the surveillance footage.

Tugging on the ends of my hair, I turned back to the board at the front of the room with the compiled information we had on the case so far. There were only two more banks in the area that had safety deposit boxes that went high enough to have a box number that they'd gone after. Which meant we had a fifty-fifty shot at figuring out what Noel was after.

"We need to make sure I'm one of the people breaking into that vault the next time he sends someone in."

"You want to do what?" Molly demanded.

"You brought me in on this case, because of my unique background and skills. Well, I think it's time I shed Kayla Rogers, FBI Agent and step back into my life as the almost-criminal who could walk through walls."

"And what exactly would your cover be?" Molly pushed back.

"We have Avery do a little backstopping for me, make it look like I've got more of a record than I actually do. Give him a reason to think I'd be worth blackmailing into taking the fall for his crime. Serena knows the type of people he goes after to do the actual dirty work. So, we make sure that whatever history we create fits that to a T." I stopped moving.

"Then, we can turn Serena loose and have her bring me in to him. Once he takes the bait and puts me on assignment, we find whatever he's after, and make sure he doesn't get it."

"You think she'd turn on him and work with us?" Duncan asked.

"You weren't the only one who noticed that brand on her wrist. And I can't say that I've ever met an Order member who'd actually managed to turn their back on the organization," Jacquie added.

"She says she wants out of that life, and I believe her. She seems like she's just scared and didn't' have anywhere to turn when someone she was supposed to be able to trust betrayed her. Honestly, if Desmond hadn't come into my life when he had, I might have ended up exactly where she is, maybe worse."

"Even if we can get a backstory built for you in time and Serena agrees to help us, how can you be so sure that you'll get picked for the right bank?" Molly pointed out.

"We know there's only two banks left, so we stake out both locations. I go in and if I don't find whatever it is he's looking for, then I let you guys know and you move on the other bank."

"That's all well and good in theory, but none of us have magic. We wouldn't be able to see anyone who was there," Duncan noted.

"If Noel sticks to his pattern, he's still only going to be hitting one bank at a time. Like I said, he's been using Serena exclusively as a lookout. I can't see him changing things up at the last minute."

"And what if he knows she's been in our custody?" Duncan continued.

"I don't think we have any other option. It's a risk we're going to have to talk<" I answered.

"All right. Get Serena onboard and bring Avery up to speed. I want this ready to go by tomorrow morning." Molly's words were authoritative, but I could still see the hint of worry in the lines around her eyes.

I was so determined to leave my past behind me, that the thought of stepping back into the person I'd been before I'd met any of these people scared me. I just had to hope the pull of who I used to be wasn't as strong as the one I'd become.

SEVENTEEN

Serena stared at me as I stood in the women's bathroom, a box of hair dye in my hand. Jacquie stood out in the hallway, ostensibly waiting to hear from Avery that my cover was in place. It had taken most of the afternoon to convince Serena to cooperate and for Avery to work her tech wizardry.

"You definitely don't look like a cop now," she offered as I toweled off my hair.

I studied my reflection in the mirror. It was a brighter purple than I'd typically gone with in the past. I'd preferred to rock the punk look, but this would have to do given our time constraints.

"I'll take that as a compliment," I said and washed my hair.

"You really think you can beat him?" she broached, turning to balance against the second small sink.

"He's going to regret ever thinking about using people's pasts against them like this." I stepped into the larger of the two toilet stalls and stripped out of my blouse and dress pants, tugging on black jeans and a midnight blue top. It almost felt as though I were a snake doing some strange shedding of its skin.

"You know, if you really meant what you said about wanting out of the Order life, there are people who can help."

"Yeah, sure. Like they'd accept a screw-up like me."

"They accepted me," I shared. "I know how scary it is when your magic takes on a mind of its own and does things you don't want. It feels like the weirdest betrayal in the world. But you don't have to let what your magic did define you. You're still a witch and you still have control over what your magic does."

"I'll think about it," she said.

Straightening my top and pulling on the leather jacket that had been like a part of me for years, I emerged from the stall. The exterior door opened, and Jacquie stepped in and offered me a smirk.

"That's the Kayla I remember from my police days."

"Please tell me we got the all-clear from Avery," I said.

"She insists she needs to triple check her work. I think she's just stalling. She knows if she doesn't hand over what she's got, we aren't sending you into the belly of the beast."

"Tell her I'll be fine," I said.

Jacquie shrugged. "Can't say I blame her for worrying about her friends rushing into dangerous situations without backup."

"I'm not running into anything without

backup. Remember you guys will have my back."

"Uh, not that I'm trying to be difficult, but what if he doesn't agree to pick you? Like I said, he's given me a list and your name isn't on it. If it just magically appeared, he'd know something is up."

She had a point. Except I had to assume that even if he was confident Kirkland had taken Corbin out of play with the prison beat-down, he still hadn't found what he was after. Also that meant he might just take a chance on a down-on-her-luck girl with a knack for slipping by surveillance systems.

"It's going to work," I said, letting a little bit of power out into the universe, hoping it would bring good things to fruition.

"Okay. Tell me again how you get in touch with him about these jobs Serena," I said as we followed Jacquie out of the bathroom and down to the back elevators. We didn't need anyone who might be watching to see her leaving with us, acting all chummy.

"He texts me a time and I meet him.

Then he gives me an address with another time, and I have to show up and keep an eye out."

"What about when you have to go recruiting? Does he give you time to do that?"

"Usually he's already picked out who he wants me to use."

"How do you know who you're supposed to be keeping an eye out for on the front end? I got the feeling from talking to Corbin he didn't know you and he's not magical."

"He always makes them wear something red. A bandana or a tie and I can always see their gun holster."

I made a mental note to double check the footage we had to see if that was actually true. I couldn't say I'd noticed anything like that on Corbin, but then again I'd been focused on trying to understand what was motivating him not to fight the charges.

"I want you to reach out to Noel. Tell him you need to meet, because you found someone you think would be good for what he's after," I said.

"I told you, he tells me what to do," she insisted.

"It's time for you to start pushing back, Serena," Jacquie said as her phone rang. She stepped away for a minute before looking at me. "We're good to go with your backstory. This better work."

I wanted to reassure her that this was going to go exactly to plan, but I wasn't stupid enough to believe that. I just had to hope it didn't completely go off the rails. I returned Serena's phone and watched her text a message.

"Tell him to meet you at Notre Dame," I coached.

Her fingers trembled and she had to erase the message twice before she got the words right and hit send. She shifted her weight as we waited for the elevator to reach the first floor. Her phone chimed with an incoming message and she looked at the screen, eyes wide.

"He actually agreed to it."

"You aren't going to be alone; I promise.

We are going to be with you the whole time," I said.

"Even if this place is crowded, he can't know you're there," she replied.

"Don't worry about that. He won't."

"You sure your bar buddy is going to be okay with us running an operation in his bar?" Jacquie whispered in my ear.

"I don't really care what he thinks," I retorted and got into the car.

NOTRE DAME WAS PACKED when we arrived. Under normal circumstances it would be a logistical nightmare to keep track of Serena and listen in on her conversation with Noel. These weren't normal circumstances though. I settled myself down at the far end of the bar so I could see most of the space. Molly settled on the stool beside me, giving me some cover if Noel happened to look this way.

"You sure you're up for this?" she pressed.

"I told you, this is why you brought me into this case in the first place. I think part of me was just waiting for that shoe to drop."

"I meant tonight. From what Jacquie told me, you looked pretty worn out and we don't need you ... I don't know, glitching."

"I'll be fine." I patted my previously injured arm. "It's already healed up and I feel better. Cliché as it sounds, J.T. really is a miracle worker."

I caught Molly eyeing a figure down at the other end of the bar. Jonathan turned, caught her looking and slung the towel he'd been using to clean glasses over his shoulder.

"We've got a positive ID outside," Jacquie's voice said from the earpiece in my ear.

I turned my attention to Serena, who lingered near a high-top table nursing a soda. She twisted the tiny straw in her fingers so fast I wouldn't have been surprised to see it go flying. We hadn't given her an earpiece or any other listening device. That's where I came in. I tugged the piece out of my own ear to avoid the distractions and focused once I spotted Noel in the crowd.

Lavender wrapped itself around me in a pocket of warmth and sweetness as I poured out my focus into the world. I needed to hear only their conversation. The ambiance of the bar faded until I could hear the thrum of Serena's heartbeat as Noel stepped up to the table beside her, a messenger bag slung crosswise over his chest.

"You have a lot of nerve telling me what to do," he growled.

"You know the cops arrested that guy yesterday," Serena said, putting just the right amount of paranoia into her tone.

"Don't tell me the little ghost is scared of getting caught," he taunted. "I told you, when the job is done, you can go back to your pathetic little life."

"And when will that be?" she pressed.

"Sooner than you think. We're close. But all you need to worry about is showing up where and when I tell you."

"I have done everything you told me to do.

I even watched that woman though she had nothing to do with any of this. I talked to her. She's just some cashier struggling to earn a decent living."

Noel leaned over the table, doing his best to act intimidating. "I told you to keep tabs only. You could have ruined everything!"

"How can I ruin everything when I don't even know what you're looking for. You say it's something powerful, but that's so vague. I'm starting to think you're just doing this, because you think it's fun to toy with people's lives."

Noel's right hand clenched into a fist. I was halfway off the barstool, ready to intervene, when his hand relaxed.

"You don't need to know what I'm looking for."

"Who am I going to tell?"

I appreciated her digging, especially when we were listening, but I didn't need her blowing her cover.

"It doesn't matter what it is. All you need to know is that we're close to finding it and once that happens, you'll be free to go," he repeated.

That seemed strange to me. If he was the one pulling all the strings, he should have an idea of what he was looking for.

"I can't keep going to the same people. Others in the group are starting to talk."

"Logistics are my department," he spat.

"Someone new started coming recently. They might be willing to help," she continued, starting to bait him.

I'd give her this, she could put on a good show when she wanted to.

"Forgive me if I don't trust your judgment," he scoffed.

"Come on, give him my name," I hissed, even though I knew she couldn't hear me.

"You can check her out, but I think you'll like what you see," Serena replied, spinning the straw in her drink again.

Noel's head swiveled side to side, as if he were looking for something or someone. I turned to face the bar in front of me to avoid him seeing my face. He didn't need to know I was privy to their conversation and I definitely didn't need him pegging me as law enforcement.

"Fine, I'll look into them and if I like what I see, I'll be in touch," he grumbled.

I glanced over my shoulder to see her pass him the slip of paper with my name on it. He pocketed it and gestured for her to leave. I tried to give Serena an encouraging nod to signal that she could leave. Jacquie was waiting for her outside.

I let the magic fade and the other sounds of the bar came flooding back, making my ears ring and my head ache. I rubbed at my temples as I tried to gauge what Noel would do next.

"That went better than expected," Molly said.

I wasn't so sure. Just because he'd taken my name didn't mean he was going to act on it. We needed him to look at my fake file and make contact. In front of me, my phone buzzed with an incoming text from Duncan. I skimmed it and said to Molly, "Looks like the people that Avery was able to identify from the surveillance footage from the bar are all parolees and probationers on Noel's caseload."

"Looks like he might be looking you up," she noted.

I turned back to see him tapping away at his phone. I couldn't be sure from this distance. I needed to get closer. The place wasn't crowded enough for me to sneak by undetected without using magic. But, there was enough of a distraction thanks to the music and dancing that pulling a disappearing act was still feasible. Jonathan didn't like people doing magic in his bar. That didn't mean it still didn't happen.

Hide me.

The scent of a dozen lavender flowers bloomed around me and wrapped me in that familiar layer of invisibility. I was careful to avoid the mass of gyrating bodies on the dance floor as I reached the table where Noel stood. From this distance, I could in fact see he'd logged in to check out my name in the database. It showed that I had just been placed on probation, but my case was unassigned. He set down the phone on the table and retrieved a small tablet from the messenger bag at his side. Tapping away at the detachable keyboard, I watched him log into the probation system and assign me to his caseload.

I tried to sense if he actually had magic, but nothing was obvious when I reached out with my supernatural senses. He felt as mundane as Corbin had. But that didn't make sense, did it? Unless he wasn't the mastermind we assumed him to be. However, all of the information and evidence we had pointed to him pulling the strings. There was still a missing link in the chain that I couldn't quite see.

I retreated as he reached for his phone again. I caught him dialing a number and I made it back to the bar in time for the burner phone I'd had Avery associate with my backstory to ring with the incoming call. I'd thought far enough ahead to put it on vibrate so at least it wouldn't blare an obnoxious ring tone. Not that I thought he'd be able to distinguish it from the other sounds around us. Still, it was better to be safe.

"Do I answer it?" I asked Molly.

"Let it go to voicemail."

I did as she instructed and watched when a few seconds later, the phone displayed both the missed call and the voicemail. I pocketed the phone, knowing we had time to listen to the message and pushed myself away from the bar. In the periphery of my vision, I watched as Noel packed up his tablet and exited the bar. I gave him a count of sixty before I tapped Molly on the shoulder and we, too, left Notre Dame behind.

Duncan met us halfway down the block. He'd apparently stepped into line to avoid being seen by Noel as he'd left the establishment. I couldn't help snickering at the fact he was still in a dress shirt and suit pants.

"I know you were trying to blend in, but you stick out like a sore thumb," I teased.

"How'd it go in there?" He didn't even respond to my jab.

"Serena did well. Got him to look me up and I saw him add me to his caseload."

"And he called her," Molly added.

I retrieved the burner phone and pressed the phone to my ear, listening to the voicemail.

"Kayla Rogers, my name is Noel Verano. I've been assigned to monitor your probation. Per the terms of your probation, you are required to meet with me. I will expect you at nine o'clock sharp tomorrow."

When I lowered the phone, I found my colleagues watching me with expectant expressions.

"He took the bait. He's expecting me tomorrow at nine."

We were closing in on this bastard now. I could almost feel the victory making my pride swell. Time to let old Kayla out to play.

JUNE 6, 2019

EIGHTEEN

I didn't sleep that night. Not because I was afraid I would be late for the meeting with Noel and make the wrong kind of first impression, but because I was still trying to piece together how he could have such control over people with power if he was mundane. I'd ended up circling the theory that Kirkland was somehow pulling the strings, but even that didn't make sense entirely. He'd been in solitary confinement and from what I'd seen of his magic, he was in complete control of his gifts. He didn't carry himself like a Whisperer, so I doubted he was walking through walls. Besides, even prisoners in solitary confinement got checked on by guards.

I was downing my second cup of coffee as I made my way to the lobby of the probation office. I'd left Duncan listening in from the car over my earpiece. I'd concealed it with some hair and a bit of magic. I had to reassure him multiple times that I would be fine.

As I took a seat, I tried to settle back in my old life. The Kayla from before Desmond and the Authority, and everything that had changed my life for the better. There had been such bitterness and anger fueling my magic back then. And sorrow at the fact that I was no longer in control. Almost like sense memory, those feelings bubbled up in my chest, burning like acid. My magic rose up, ready to hide me away from the world.

No, not yet.

The time for displays would come. I needed to let him know that I had power and wasn't afraid to use it. Though I needed him to think he had the upper hand. Still, sitting in those emotions again was more draining than

I'd expected and I felt tears sting the backs of my eyes.

The receptionist sitting behind the desk looked up from her computer screen long enough to push a box of tissues toward me without a word.

"Thanks," I sniffed, dabbing at my eyes so as not to ruin the mascara and eyeliner I'd applied.

"Better you don't go in there crying," the woman said, glancing toward the door with a name plate reading Noel Verano.

I pocketed the tissue then straightened as the door opened and Noel strode out. He looked at me with a bit of surprise. Maybe he'd assumed I wouldn't be punctual and hoped he could chide me for attendance. I wasn't going to give him an inch.

"Come in," he said, stepping back into the office enough for me to pass him.

The interior of the office was what I would call office neutral. It had beige walls and a dark wooden bookcase along the far wall. Thick books sat on the shelves, but I highly doubted he'd ever read them. They were for show. It's what anyone would expect walking into the office of a state employee.

Noel closed the door and moved to sit across from me. He opened up a thick file—Jeez Avery—and thumbed through some papers clipped to the left interior of the folder. "So, you're on probation for repeat shoplifting and vandalism, Ms. Rogers. Although given your record, I'd say you must have a guardian angel. I would have expected to see some jail time awaiting you."

"Guess I got lucky," I replied.

"We'll see about that," he countered dismissively. "You understand the terms of this arrangement? You are to check-in with me about finding housing and employment. If I so much as catch wind of you sticking a single toe out of line, the court is going to revoke your probation and you will be seeing the inside of a jail cell."

He leaned forward; lips set in a terse expression. If he thought I was intimidated, he was horribly mistaken. Even if he'd actually been my probation officer years ago, Noel wouldn't have scared me.

"Yeah, I get it," I answered, waving a hand to show just how much I didn't care.

"Tell me, how was it you could walk away with thousands of dollars in stolen watches without being seen?"

I flashed back to the petty theft of my college years. It had been so easy to just slip in unnoticed and take whatever caught my fancy. It wasn't until I'd started working with other people that I risked getting caught.

"I'm very creative," I replied.

He shook his head and laughed. "Creativity my ass. You've got magic."

The bluntness of his statement caught me off guard. I pressed myself against the back of the chair and my hands gripped the armrests. "I don't ..." My brain stalled out as I tried to recover.

"Acknowledge it. We need him to rope you in," Duncan's voice whispered in the hidden earpiece in my ear.

"You know about that stuff?" I relaxed my grip.

"You'd be surprised what I know," he sneered. "I'm guessing you don't have any trouble sneaking in and out of places unseen for good reason."

"Look, I'm paying my debt. I'll show up and do whatever check-ins you want. I just … can you maybe not put it on blast that I'm, you know … different?"

"I have a little job I need done and I think you're the perfect person for it," he said, standing and moving to lean over me. I could feel his breath against my skin and I couldn't hide the impulse to recoil from him.

"What sort of job?"

"Nothing you haven't done before. I just need you to walk in, open a box, and take what's inside, as long as it's confirmed magical."

"What sort of box?"

"A safety deposit box," he replied. "That isn't a problem is it?"

"Usually those need keys," I reminded him.

"Walking through walls is no problem for you, I don't see why a little lock on a box would be a problem either."

"What exactly am I supposed to be looking for?"

"Oh, that's for me to worry about."

"But how do I know I've got the right stuff?"

"You can feel other people's magic right?"

"Sometimes. I don't go around looking for other people. I just try to keep to myself. Other people's magic getting involved makes things too messy for my taste."

"I have every confidence you'll manage what I'm asking," he said.

"And if I say no?"

"Your pretty punk ass will wind up behind bars faster than you can say abracadabra," he replied gruffly.

"Even if I haven't done anything wrong?" I pressed.

He pushed away from the chair so forcefully it tipped and fell on the back two legs. Out of self-preservation lavender-tinted tendrils of magic shot from my hands down to the floor, levering me to a sturdy position.

"Don't forget that I own you now. You do what I tell you and it's all glowing reports," he said.

"So, where am I supposed to go?"

"I'll text you the details. Be ready. It happens this afternoon." He gestured to the door. "Now, get out."

My magic strengthened around me. It didn't like his tone and neither did I. In the back of my head, I was begging him to make a move toward me so I could lay him out. I'd do it without leaving a mark. It would be so easy.

"I said get out," Noel boomed.

I waited until I was outside of the office building to speak. "I cannot wait to take that manipulative piece of shit down."

"Patience, partner," Duncan said in my ear. "Time to get ready for a bank heist."

TRUE TO HIS WORD, by two o'clock, I'd received a text from Noel with a street address and a box number: 664. Just like all the other banks he'd forced people to hit. He followed up the message with a time: 2:45 p.m.

"We're a go," I announced to the other occupants of the conference room at FBI headquarters.

I passed the phone to Jacquie who compared the address to the ones left on our list. She pointed to a little blue pin on the map of the city. There was one other blue pin out near the airport and the aquarium.

"He still hasn't told you what he's after?" she said.

"Nope. Just that's it's magical and I should be able to feel it. I don't know how he thinks I'm going to do that. I mean, yeah my magic is potent when it wants to be, but it's not like I've trained for that sort of thing."

"Well, we're going to have to hope you know what's up. As soon as you get into the vault, you need to let us know what you find," Molly said.

"I know the plan," I replied.

My burner phone beeped with another message, this time from Serena. We'd ensured she had the number in case Noel reached out to her again. It was a brief message: *See you soon.*

Either she already knew we had the same address or she was hoping that he would stick to his pattern and only hit one bank at a time. As we headed for the SUV parked out front, I tried to go over everything I knew about Noel and Kirkland, and what might motivate them to plan these heists.

It wasn't that I assumed everything horrible happened on some sort of cosmic timetable, but in my experience, the bad guys tended to make their big moves at the most inopportune times for us good guys. The solstice was still weeks away and even now, good magic had a slight advantage as the balance of power shifted back our way.

"Agent Rogers, did you hear me?" Jacquie called, snapping her fingers in front of my face.

"What? Sorry, I was thinking."

"You're going to need to leave your weapon here."

I was starting to grow used to having it on me and taking off the holster felt almost as if I was naked. Except she was right. Kayla Rogers, loner with a criminal history wouldn't have access to a gun, let alone an FBI issued sidearm. So, I unclipped the holster and passed it to Jacquie.

"You've got this," she coached as the clock on the car's dashboard clicked over to 2:37.

I didn't pay much attention to where we were heading until the car pulled up a block away from the bank. It was downtown, not far from the Boston Public Library and several MBTA transit lines. Something about the place felt vaguely familiar. Though I couldn't place why and didn't have time to stand around and wonder. I had a bank to infiltrate. It would have been easier if I had any idea where the vault and security boxes were located.

"Psst," Serena's voice caught my attention

I strolled past the front of the bank and turned down the side street running perpendicular to the entrance.

"Please tell me that he gave you more information than just a place and a time," I said, pressing my body closer to the building. We weren't invisible yet and there were plenty of security cameras in the area.

Serena held up her phone with a tiny map of the interior of the bank with a tiny red circle which I interpreted as my destination. I plucked the phone from her hands and studied the schematic. It looked like the wall we were standing next to connected the interior to the ATMs and the lobby. I didn't really want to wind up stuck in a machine if my magic decided to revolt on me.

"Do we know who is supposed to be distracting the staff up front?" I scanned the people walking by. None of them stood out as carrying concealed weapons or wearing a splash of red.

"Not yet."

"Damn. The easiest way in would be

through the front door, but I can't be seen entering that way. Trailing our third wheel would have been ideal." I studied the blueprint on the screen again. The bank's walls went back farther down the street leading into what appeared to be an office or closet space. That would be easier to get through.

"I'm going back there. See you on the other side," I said and jogged down the street.

"You guys still with me?" I whispered.

"Read you loud and clear," Duncan answered.

"Team Two is in position at the other location, ready to roll on your word, Agent Rogers," an unfamiliar male voice replied.

"You can do this," I breathed, trying to convince myself that I wasn't about to go walking into a trap.

Instead of just letting my magic pool around me to get me through, I reached into the world, seeking out any connection I could find with the natural forces that were a part of this interconnected web of power. *Give me the strength to do this.*

Magic swirled around me, bumping up against my body like a cat trying to give affection. I let it envelope me before I unleashed my own magic. This was what my magic was used to, the need to move about unseen. Finger by finger, my hands vanished as the invisibility cascaded up my arms, past my elbows until it had erased all of me. I pressed an invisible hand against the concrete wall in front of me and pushed.

The molecules parted for me as if I were Moses conducting the Red Sea to allow passage out of Egypt. I held my breath as I stepped through and into the office on the other side. Thankfully, it was vacant when I emerged. I was about to take a step forward when I heard someone shout and caught the word 'gun.' Now was the time to see what was so precious and stowed in box 664.

Despite the fact no one could see me, I darted into the hallway and quickly found the vault. It was really more of a large closet with a keypad lock on the door. Passing through the door was easier than the exterior wall and I let out a breath when I made it into the room. I spun in a slow circle, taking in the numbered boxes until I spotted the box in question.

"Let's see what's so special about you," I said and pressed a hand to the lock. I poured out a little extra will, making it clear that I needed to get inside that box.

The lock disengaged and the box came loose. I backpedaled to the small table at the center of the room and flipped it open. It appeared to be an odd collection of random objects, like someone's family heirlooms.

"Anything?" Duncan's voice crackled in my earpiece.

"Maybe," I answered.

I picked up a medallion that sat at the top of the pile and studied it. It didn't seem like it should be important to a thug doing time in prison or a corrupt parole officer. *What am I missing?*

Noel had told me I would know if the contents were magical. Time to test that theory. I let out a little of my power, feeling it wrap around the medallion in my hand. The scent of lavender was immediately overpowered by a different scent—strawberry.

Oh. Oh no.

"I found it," I said, hoping Duncan could hear me. Without realizing it, my protective barrier of magic vanished.

White noise and static were my only response as I heard heavy breathing behind me. I spun to find Kirkland standing opposite me.

"I know you," he said and swung his meaty fist at my head.

NINETEEN

Unlike the first time he'd come for me in his little mind palace, I was fast enough to dodge the blow. His fist slammed into Box 662 with a painful sounding crunch.

"You're supposed to be in solitary confinement, Nicky," I replied, pocketing the medallion and the other items as discreetly as I could.

"And you're a cop," he snarled.

"FBI if we're being technical," I replied.

"You think you're so clever, getting in my head like that, you sneaky little ghost."

"You know, I'm starting to find the word ghost offensive," I retorted. Stepping toward the still-locked door. Which made me wonder, how had he gotten in?

"I told him using people like you would backfire. You all think you're fucking untouchable."

"I can understand you being involved in this. I mean, I guess being wrapped up in the Order like you were, was a hard thing to give up," I said, hoping that by keeping him talking, the team would realize something had gone wrong.

"You don't know anything about them," he growled. Tendrils of white-hot electricity rippled along his forearms, pooling in his palm like it had in his mind.

At least he was consistent.

Time seemed to slow as my brain finally sorted through the pieces that had been missing. Whether Noel had known for certain what was in the box, he'd known enough to be able to tell the people he coerced to check for defensive magic. Maybe since the practitioner who'd placed protection on the medallion I'd picked up had been a friend and somehow recognized my specific magic or because I hadn't actually intended to do it harm, it hadn't fought me. Though I could imagine in the wrong hands, it could pack a real punch. I could work with that.

"I know that your bosses got themselves wiped off the map, because of their stupidity and lust for power. And from where I'm standing, you're not much better. Hell, you're going to end up in prison for the rest of your life after this."

"No one on the inside is going to bat an eye for me killing a cop."

"Yeah, but I bet the warden is going to want an explanation for how you escaped solitary. Humor me, how'd you do it?"

Kirkland's jaw worked, as if chewing on his words. "Borrowed a trick out of your book and walked through some walls."

"Not as easy as it looks," I commented.

"And what about Noel? We know he's been your visitation buddy for months."

""He likes to think he's important but he's expendable, too."

"What, did you tell him to go pay you a visit while you pulled your Houdini act?"

"Something like that."

At least I knew I could get Noel for conspiracy and aiding in a prison break, if nothing else. "I'd hate to be in his shoes. And you know, for someone who talks shit about Whisperers, you sure didn't have a problem using their brand of magic for your own gain."

The electricity he'd been building jumped out of his hand and launched at my chest. A silvery barrier materialized in front of me, deflecting the blast into the ground where it would do the least amount of harm. I could hear alarms beginning to sound in the bank beyond us. Either we'd managed to set off some sort of warning system or the police were responding to Noel's distraction.

He didn't give me time to recover before he lobbed an energy sphere at the ceiling, letting it come crashing down beyond the boundaries of my barrier. I was about to let out a laugh at his poor aim when the energy ball exploded, sending me slamming back against the door to the outside. I felt something crunch painfully in my side and every breath hurt.

Fuck, I think he broke a rib.

Like I'd done in Noel's office, I let my magic solidify into thick ropes. They snaked along the floor, wrapping right around his right foot before I pulled hard and sent him toppling to the ground.

"Do you even know what the stuff is you're trying to steal?" I yelled, inching another step toward the door.

"Do you?" he countered.

All I knew was that years ago, Ezri had taken measures to protect the ancestral magic of the members of the Council. She'd secreted away the protection and hadn't told a soul. At least not one living. How he'd managed to get that information I had no idea.

"Come on, tell me how you figured it out.

That's the one piece of the puzzle I can't determine," I said, hoping his superiority complex would kick in and he'd fill in the blank for me.

"You'd be surprised the kind of information you can pry out of people when they think no one's listening. Stupid woman let it slip about how her family's power was protected."

"So, you knew about the objects. That doesn't explain the box number," I prodded.

"That's on Noel. He hacked into some database, found her name, and box number, but got caught before he figured out which bank it was. He made up for that by orchestrating this little show."

"You honestly think you're going to be able to do anything with these things? They're not meant for you or your buddy Noel." Putting on a brave face when every breath felt like I was swallowing fire was exhausting. The edges of my vision grew hazy and gray, somehow I stayed on my feet.

Kirkland stepped closer to the barrier that separated us and reached out a finger. He touched the very edge of the barrier and smoke filled my nostrils. The barrier faltered before sputtering out.

"Did you forget the first rule of magic? All it takes is a little intent to sway magic. Just one touch and what was once protected, will now be undone."

He reached for the pocket of my jacket, but I spun out of his reach. "Two can play that game," I replied, sounding far more confident than I was.

If you can hear me, I need your help. I need to borrow your protective magic.

I let out a gasp as a new sensation hit me. It was like someone else was temporarily in control of my body. My fingers moved of their own accord and the usual smell of lavender was sweetened by her power. And then it wasn't just within me, but all around me. It tinted the currents of magic with a faint red hue and I reached for it, letting it fuel me as I threw up another barrier, this one reaching to the ceiling.

"Fighting is pointless. I'm going to get

what I want and they will have no choice but to bow to me."

"No one is going to bow to a loser like you," I retorted.

All of the anger and frustration I'd felt over the last few days bubbled over inside of me. I finally had a target for those emotions and I let it fuel the magic within me. The power formed into incorporeal fists, lashing out beyond the barrier, sending him staggering backwards into the far wall.

"Why Noel Verano?" I asked, closing the gap between us. "He's a thug of a different sort, but he doesn't have magic. I thought the Order was above dealing with mundane people."

"Every strong ruler needs foot soldiers ready to do as they are asked, no matter the consequences. He was a convenient partnership."

"You helped funnel him potential pawns in your sick little treasure hunt, not caring what he threatened them with to stay in line."

"Our plan was solid," he argued.

"Except, why bother with the front man distraction? If you really just wanted to get into the vaults, why not just use the Whisperers? You'd never even leave a trail."

His jaw worked, but he couldn't come up with an answer.

"You just didn't care, did you?" The magical extensions of my hands reached out and pinned him back against the wall.

I could see his eyes starting to bulge in his head and he clawed at the manifestation of my power. Everything inside of me wanted to see him hurt like the people he and Noel had forced into their sick pursuit of power.

"Stand down."

It was like she was standing there next to me. I turned, but no one was there. Had it just been in my head or was the presence and strength of her power, even after all these years later, playing tricks on my mind.

I blinked as I tried to clear the confusion in my head. It didn't matter whether I was hallucinating it or if the sheer amount of magic around me was urging me in the one way it knew I'd respond to.

I let the magic fall away and backed up toward the door. The contents of the safety deposit box clinked within my pocket. "You are done, Kirkland. You and Noel."

"You're no one. You're all just echoes of who you used to be. Your only power is disappearing," he spat at me in a last ditch attempt to insult me.

"That's where you're wrong. We are stronger than you could ever realize. We've faced one of the hardest parts of living with magic and we've come out the other side. We may have the ability to hide from the world, but it is our choice when we are seen. And no matter what happens, we will always have that choice. That freedom to reclaim our place in the world."

I turned, my hand on the door handle. "But you, you're not going to have that option, because you couldn't let old grudges die. You wanted to take hold of that power and corrupt it, because you thought you could. Magic has consequences, Nicholas. And this is yours."

I pulled the door open to find Duncan standing on the other side of the threshold, gun ready. The moment our eyes locked, he lowered his weapon and pulled me into a tight embrace. The strangled cry of pain that came out of my mouth made him release me immediately.

"We lost comms. What happened?"

"We had a party crasher," I wheezed, pressing my hand to my side. I could definitely feel bone protruding. "We probably ought to get him back to prison and scoop up Noel Verano while we're at it. We've got enough to charge them both with orchestrating the robberies."

Duncan stepped into the room and hauled Kirkland to his feet. I followed the line of security personnel back to the front of the bank and out onto the street. I spotted Serena halfway down the block, flanked by Molly and Jacquie.

"You got him?" Serena said, tugging on

the sleeve of her hoodie to cover the mark she still bore.

"Both of them. They aren't going to be hurting anyone ever again."

"Please tell me we got what he was after?" Molly said.

I patted my pocket. "I finally understand what this was about. I'll fill you in back at headquarters. But first, I need a hospital."

BEING friends with a healer who had a penchant for listening to incoming ambulance calls came in handy. J.T. stepped out of the ambulance that pulled up to the bank and ushered me inside. I eased my jacket off, so he could examine me.

"Just because she inspired you to go into this line of work doesn't mean you have to be as careless as she was about her personal safety," J.T. chastised as he pressed a honey-scented bandage to my ribcage.

"I didn't mean to get so banged up," I replied.

"Here, lay back," he urged and continued to check me over. "Well, on the plus side it doesn't sound like you punctured a lung."

I gave him a thumbs up. "I could feel her in there. It was like she was with me."

"I'd like to say you were just hallucinating from pain, but I know that magic has a funny way of showing up just when you need it most."

The rest of the ride to the hospital was a haze as he forced an oxygen mask on me that tasted suspiciously of his magic. On arrival, a nurse ushered me to a private room and shortly thereafter, the rest of my team traipsed in.

"So, you want to fill us in?" Jacquie said.

The nurse had insisted I remove my jacket, so she could put monitoring leads on me. I gestured to it sitting on the chair beside the bed. She emptied the contents on the foot of the bed.

"This may sound like a dumb question, but

how do you know that's what they were after?"

"Because I could feel the magic tied to these things. Lots of different signatures. They all had a little bit of one common thread in them, though," I replied, eyeing Jacquie and Molly. They'd been involved with that case.

"They were trying to take out the rest of the Council?" Jacquie hissed.

I struggled to sit up in the bed without grimacing too hard. J.T. might be magic, but even his power took time to work. "I don't know. But Kirkland managed to dispel a barrier I'd put up with just a touch. I don't want to think about what he could have done if he'd gotten his hands on them. For all we know, he could have somehow corrupted the magic in those bloodlines. Or eliminated them altogether."

"Well, whatever he had planned, it's not happening now," Molly replied.

If we had our way, he and his co-conspirator would stay in prison for a long time. "We know that the people they roped into this were coerced. I'm not letting them get dragged down for this. I'm going to make sure they all get deals and leniency."

I'd seen what getting wrapped up in the magical machinations of a madman had done to Kevin. I owed it to him to break that cycle, to let that be the start of my legacy.

JUNE 7, 2019

TWENTY

I expected every part of me to ache when I woke the next morning, and yet, I felt the most rested I had in months. I'd made it. I'd survived my first case and the bad guys would be going away for a long time. I sat up, kicked the blankets off and stopped short. I realized in that moment the people I most wanted to tell about this success were the ones who were no longer around to hear it. At least not in the way I would have liked.

That didn't stop me from sharing the news anyway. I suspected a few other people might want to share in the celebration, too. Sending a quick text to a hastily compiled group chat, I headed for the bathroom, ready to get the purple dye out of my hair. It had been such a large part of my identity for so long that the thought of abandoning it when I entered the academy had seemed nearly impossible. Now, I was eager to put that part of my past behind me. I could still acknowledge the piece of me that was her and how that had helped me, too. Only now I was ready to fully embrace who I had become in the wake of everything.

A capable agent and a stronger witch. Like Ezri, I was learning to surround myself with people I could trust. People I didn't have to hide from and who had my back, because they knew I had theirs.

Twenty minutes later, I emerged with just the barest hint of purple at the roots of my hair, ready to face whatever was coming next. I was halfway out the door when my phone rang, showing an unfamiliar number.

"Hello?"

"Kayla, it's your mom."

The panic that had filled me only days ago

ebbed slightly. She was trying to be in my life, and it was up to me to either let her in or keep her out. I'd spent so much of my adulthood keeping her at arm's length, it was still difficult to fathom letting her into my world. Despite that, she needed someone to show her the ropes of existing as a Whisperer. My guide on that journey had nearly steered me into a life I would regret. The least I could do was give my mom the chance to prove she wanted to be better.

"Everything okay?" I finally replied, fishing my keys from my purse and locking my apartment door.

"Oh, yes. I just wanted to call and say thank you. I can't tell you how much it meant that you let me back into your life."

"I'm trying to let the past heal and move on. And that means accepting what happened between us and try to build something new. I can't promise that it's going to be easy."

"I know. I made things harder on you, because I was too scared to face my own demons. I realize now that I drove you away and I'm the reason your magic turned on you."

"If it hadn't, I don't think I'd be where I am today. So, as shitty as it was in the moment, I think it needed to happen."

"Well, I'm still sorry I put you through that."

"If you want, I can probably show you some tricks of the trade with your magic. I know it's hard to control when it first happens."

"I'd like that."

"And maybe you could start going back to the Authority. They're more open and accepting now. I know there's a healer there who would be more than happy to help you."

"I'll think about it."

"Good." My feet thudded on pavement as I made my way outside. "Look, I'm sorry to cut this short, but I am meeting up with some people so I need to go."

"Oh, sure. Maybe we could try doing coffee sometime soon?"

"I'd like that."

"Me, too. Call me whenever you're free."

"I will. Bye, Mom."

I hung up and turned my attention to the walk ahead. The sun was already cresting over the treetops as I reached the gated entrance to the cemetery. It was late enough in the morning that they were open and I could see someone had already opened one of the gates and ventured inside. Moving through the graves in full view of the cameras, the world felt oddly freeing as I made my way to the pair of headstones.

Jacquie was already waiting there. "She would be proud of you," she said when she spotted me. "They both would."

"I really hope so," I replied.

A pair of low voices drew my attention before I could say anything else and I turned to see Molly followed by Duncan who carried a travel tray of coffee cups. I accepted the cup he handed me.

"So, this is her?" He gestured to the closer headstone.

"I think you would have liked her. I mean,

she was kind of a douche when we first met, but she grew on me," I explained.

"She was a good cop," Molly said.

"And a selfless witch," I added.

"There are a lot more people like you out there," Duncan commented. "People with this gift that are trying to do good and make the world better."

"Yeah, there are. I don't know if we are doing the best job at it, but we are trying every day."

"She knew it wouldn't be easy and that even when we thought we'd won, there would still be evil left to fight," J.T.'s voice came off to my right. He stopped to stand in front of the second headstone.

"I guess I had hoped it wouldn't be the Order. I would have thought they realized when their entire organization got dismantled from within, that it was time to quit organized chaos," I sighed.

"Evil wears a lot of faces. And it did take them two years to even think about rearing their ugly heads. That has to mean something," Jacquie offered.

"It just makes me wonder who else is out there that we don't know about. At least with them, we had information and background on what to expect."

"Whatever comes next, we'll figure it out together," Duncan said, pressing a hand to my shoulder.

"Thanks. You don't know how much that means to me."

"I'm beginning to," he replied with a small smile.

I turned to J.T. and said, "You might be getting someone new dropping by headquarters looking for some support dealing with their magic turning on them."

"I'll do whatever I can to help." He turned his gaze to the headstone in front of him. "I know I'm a poor substitute for the work he did, but I really do believe I can make a difference, given time."

"I know everyone is grateful for you stepping up." I paused before adding, "Just so you know, it's my mom."

"Oh. That's kind of a big deal," he said.

I hadn't been nearly as close with J.T. as I had been to Desmond, but they were connected by their own shared history and it didn't surprise me that they'd talked about me. I hadn't forbidden Des from sharing my past with people and in a way I could see why it might be relevant to J.T. Healing physical maladies was one thing. Healing mental and emotional wounds was a far harder skill to master.

I reached into my purse and retrieved the evidence bag full of items we'd recovered from the safety deposit box. "I know these were locked up for a reason, but I think maybe they should find another home. One that's less accessible."

He took the bag and shifted the items within, a sad smile ghosting over his lips. "I never thought I'd see this again. Part of me didn't want to believe that I could still feel her tethered to this stuff, but it's like she's wrapping her arms around me, keeping me safe."

Magic was an amazing gift with many wonderous secrets I still didn't fully understand. How it could linger after someone was gone was one such mystery I didn't understand. Especially when as we had recently come to understand it, a person's magic could reconstitute in someone else. But maybe her role and her sacrifice had been so big that the universe hadn't called in that particular chip just yet.

"You know there is one thing you had over her," he said with a laugh, gesturing to the second headstone.

"Yeah, what's that?"

"I'm pretty sure you won't have long-dead relatives foisting or fixing their problems onto you. And it probably means there's less chance of you taking a magical bullet for the team."

I could appreciate not having the weight of being the Savior on my plate. I'd never wanted that sort of attention and expectation on me.

Though I still wasn't entirely convinced my magic wouldn't one day try to revolt against my carefully practiced grip on it.

"I know this probably seems stupid to everyone, but I'm really glad you all came. I just wanted to celebrate the win with the people who would appreciate it most," I said, clutching my coffee cup tight between my hands.

"You are honoring their legacy more than you know," Jacquie said, holding up her own cup for a toast.

I clung to her kind words as the people around me all raised their cups and we toasted to a job well done. And yet, even as we basked in the brightness of the day and the fact we had once again protected the magical community from horrific assault, I couldn't shake the feeling that the fight was just beginning.

As I stood there on hallowed ground, the tiny hairs on the back of my arms bristled, warning of some unknown danger. I did my best to pivot without looking too obvious and let out a little of my power, pushing against the magic around me to see if anything pushed back. Nothing obvious jumped out at me and I kept the feeling to myself. There was still evil in the world and we would be there to fight it, no matter what form it took.

QUICK AUTHOR'S NOTE

I HAD SO much fun getting back into the Seasons of Magic 'verse with this book. It felt so familiar to be able to step into the world and the way magic operated. I always knew that I wasn't done with this world and these characters, especially since Ezri's journey in the main series was so focused on her fate as the Savior. There were so many side characters I wanted to know more about and the way things were left at the end of Winter's Reckoning, I knew this was the perfect way to take things.

When I was conceiving this series around

Kayla, I knew I wanted her checkered past to come into play but I also wanted to have it tie more tightly into events from the main series as well. Kayla spends quite a bit of time in this book contemplating whether she can live up to Ezri's example and I really felt it was important for her to find that connection to her mentor.

But, delving into character backstory isn't finished here. I've always loved Jacquie, the no-nonsense woman who steps up to the plate whenever she's needed. But she has some tragedy in her past that ties directly into the magical community and that will be the focus on the next book.

TURN the page to get a glimpse at *Unspoken Magic*...

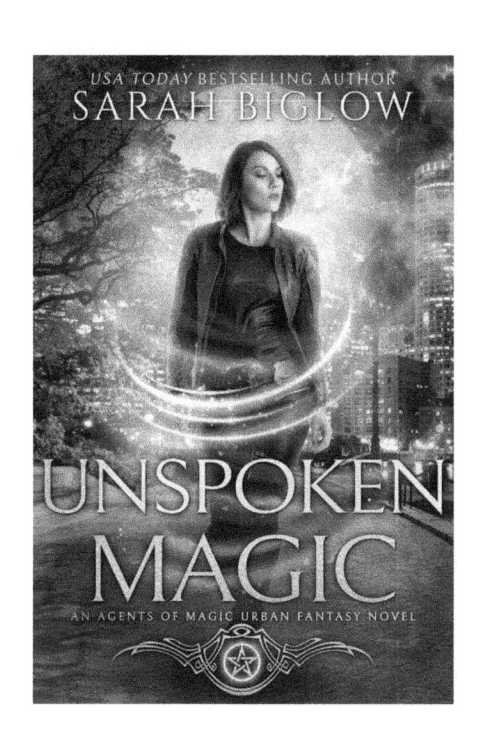

Unspoken Magic

Sometimes the past is impossible to outrun.

Agent Kayla Rogers may have survived the brush with her sordid past, but hers isn't the only past coming back to haunt her team.

When bodies begin dropping with connections to Jacquie DeWitt's deceased brother and

UNSPOKEN MAGIC BLURB

magic, the stoic agent's life turns upside down. it's up to Kayla and her team to hunt down the killer and put a stop to the dangerous magics being unleashed.

Unspoken Magic *is available for pre-order on all storefronts - find it on your favorite store today!*

ABOUT THE AUTHOR

Sarah Biglow is a *USA Today* bestselling author. She lives in Massachusetts with her husband and son. She is a licensed attorney and spends her days combatting employment discrimination as an Investigator with the

Massachusetts Commission Against Discrimination.

You can find an up-to-date list of all my books here